Praise for *Here to Stay*:

"A powerful YA novel about identity and prejudice."
—*Entertainment Weekly*

"With humor, power, smarts, and honesty, Farizan has written a conversation-starter." —*The Boston Globe*

"*Here to Stay* tackles serious, timely issues with grace, humor, and urgency." —*HelloGiggles*

"An engaging page-turner. Powerful." —*Kirkus Reviews*

"Islamophobia, racism, homo- and heterosexuality, toxic masculinity, offensive sports mascots, activism, friendship, immigration, school politics, gun rights, and a splash of Iranian history make this about a lot more than high-school sports." —*Booklist*

"*Here to Stay* is refreshingly frank, revealing the unsettling truth that the very social stigmas we pretend we have conquered still exist." —*Salisbury* (NC) *Post*

ALSO BY SARA FARIZAN

If You Could Be Mine

Tell Me Again How a Crush Should Feel

HERE TO STAY

SARA FARIZAN

ALGONQUIN 2019

Published by Algonquin Young Readers
an imprint of Algonquin Books of Chapel Hill
Post Office Box 2225
Chapel Hill, North Carolina 27515-2225

a division of Workman Publishing
225 Varick Street
New York, New York 10014

First paperback edition, Algonquin Young Readers, October 2019. Originally
published in hardcover by Algonquin Young Readers in September 2018.
Printed in the United States of America.
Published simultaneously in Canada by Thomas Allen & Son Limited.
Design by Neil Swaab.

Library of Congress Cataloging-in-Publication Data

Names: Farizan, Sara, author.
Title: Here to stay / Sara Farizan.
Description: First edition. | Chapel Hill, North Carolina : Algonquin Young
Readers, 2018. | Summary: When a cyberbully sends the entire high school
a picture of basketball hero Bijan Majidi, photo-shopped to look like a
terrorist, the school administration promises to find and punish the culprit,
but Bijan just wants to pretend the incident never happened and move on.
Identifiers: LCCN 2018008382 | ISBN 9781616207007
(hardcover : alk. paper)
Subjects: LCSH: Arab Americans—Juvenile fiction. | CYAC: Arab
Americans—Fiction. | Cyberbullying—Fiction. | Bullying—Fiction. |
Basketball—Fiction. | High schools—Fiction. | Schools—Fiction.
Classification: LCC PZ7.F179 He 2018 | DDC [Fic]—dc23
LC record available at https://lccn.loc.gov/2018008382

ISBN 978-1-61620-985-8 (PB)

10 9 8 7 6 5 4 3 2 1
First Paperback Edition

For my beautiful grandmother, Ashraf

CHAPTER ONE

"Damn," Coach Johnson muttered. "That's four fouls, Drew!" he shouted to our King James. "B, you're in." This is where all the trouble started. I sometimes wonder what would have happened if Drew had never fouled out.

I had it in my head that if I became popular, every day would feel like my birthday. I'd have no trouble talking to girls and I'd be admired by my peers at the Granger School. I did *not* think everything would turn to crap salad in a bucket.

Who could blame me? I mean, in all the movies and TV shows, the popular kid who ascends from the depths of dorkdom has their day in the sun, and then it's smooth sailing. Marty McFly gets the awesome truck. Daniel LaRusso gets to crane-kick the crap out of Johnny. Seth Rogen gets to spend time with a girl *way* out of his league in every Judd Apatow movie. But my name isn't Marty or Daniel or Seth. My name is Bijan, and the world won't let me be the hero in my own damn life.

I jumped up to check in at the scorers' table and the horn blared for substitutions. I was trying to look tough and hard, but inside I was freaking out the same way I did when my imaginary future ex-girlfriend, Elle, walked by me in the halls: so excited that I might hurl chunks all over the floor.

I jogged over to Drew and reached out to give him a low five. We barely clapped hands. Drew stared at the floor, fuming as he hustled to the bench. He wasn't supposed to foul out of a game that would determine whether our season ended or kept going. He also wasn't supposed to let me, a nonentity on loan from JV, fill in for him.

The Granger crowd was quiet as my sneakers squeaked onto the court, except for my mom and my best buddy, Sean. He stood up and yelled, "Go get 'em, Tiger!" with 1950s irony while my mom clapped and whooped next to him. She knew how much playing meant to me. She was maybe the only one in that gym besides Sean who did.

It was the beginning of the fourth quarter, Carter Prep 54, Granger 38. I joined the others around the key, waiting for the Carter Prep student to shoot his second free throw. He made the basket, the swish of the net prompting loud cheers from the visiting team's fans.

I grabbed the ball from under the basket and inbounded it to Marcus Silva, the cocaptain, who dribbled it down the court. Marcus was the only reason we had as many points as we did, and Carter Prep knew it. Their defenders were double-teaming him.

"Beej!" Marcus yelled as he passed the ball to me.

I looked to Will, but he was covered. Steve was cutting behind the basket to lose his man.

Todd was struggling to stay upright against the opposing center, who kept shoving him from behind. The shot clock was winding down. I bent my knees to shoot.

The ball hit the backboard before it went in. The Granger crowd cheered, waving the blue-and-gold plastic pom-poms the school had given out before the big game.

Our team started to run back on defense, but I was so amped I stayed behind to guard the player inbounding the ball. I hopped in front of him, waving my arms in the air.

"Back off, benchwarmer," he grunted as he tried a ball fake.

I didn't bite. Marcus doubled back. He stuck to the point guard, who was trying to receive the pass. A short, shrill whistle blew.

"Five-second violation," the official said, taking the ball.

"I do love that rule." I grinned at the scowling Carter Prep player. "If I was in *your* lofty position, I would have called a time-out. But hey, what do I know?"

The ref handed me the rock and blew the whistle again. The clock started. I inbounded to Marcus before I bolted to the top of the key to set a pick for Todd. I crisscrossed my arms flat across my chest and blocked the Carter Prep goon with my whole body, allowing Todd to cut to the hole. The Carter Prep goon guarding him crashed into me. I stumbled backward, but it was enough time for Marcus to lob a pass to Todd for an easy layup.

The crowd cheered louder, but not loud enough that I couldn't hear my mom yell.

"It's not ice hockey, Carter! Watch the checking!" Mom shouted.

"Would you listen to that crowd, Reggie? They have really come alive in this last quarter!"

Sometimes, when I need a minute, I like to pretend that Reggie Miller and Kevin Harlan, my favorite NBA commentators, give color commentary for my life.

"Well, the Granger Gunners are finally giving the crowd something to cheer about, Kevin. When you start playing with a little fire in your belly, the atmosphere completely changes."

"There is a steal from Marcus Silva, who rockets the ball over to newcomer Bijan Majidi for a three-pointer . . . BANG! He makes it! Where did this kid come from?"

"This is why I love basketball, Kevin. Anything can happen!"

I panted as I looked up at how much time we had on the clock. We were down by two with fifteen seconds left. Todd had finally been able to post up effectively and get some layups in. Will had driven to the hoop when Marcus or I were double-teamed. There was sweat running down Coach Johnson's cheeks during our time-out huddle; his sports coat was off and his armpits were soaked. He'd been sweating a lot this season. His team wasn't up to the usual Granger standards of excellence.

Coach drew up a play on his clipboard. "Okay, we've got no time-outs left. Worse comes to worst, they get the last possession, you foul," he said. "Get the ball to Marcus for the play to work. Got it?"

The buzzer sounded. I hustled to the baseline. The ref handed me the ball and then blew his whistle.

The other team didn't let Marcus breathe. A player stuck to either side of him, anticipating his every move. Marcus tried to break free, but I didn't have time to wait. I hurled the ball over my head to Will. Will drove to the hoop. As the big goon in the key moved up to guard him, Will bounce-passed to Todd, who was free under the basket.

For a split second, Todd looked terrified. The clock was winding down. Ten seconds left.

"Shoot it!" Marcus yelled. Todd tossed it up. The ball bounced twice on the rim before falling in.

"Unnnn-believable, Kevin!"

"The Granger Gunners have stunned everyone today with a comeback for the books!"

"Well, not really. I mean, it was only a sixteen-point deficit. Also, since when are prep school games in our contracts? I need to talk to my agent about this."

"Don't give them any space! Full-court press!" Marcus shouted.

The ball was inbounded to my guy. *Don't reach*, I thought. The last thing I wanted was to foul with five seconds left on the clock. Even if he made the free throws, we'd barely have time to get a final shot up. I took a deep breath and kept my hands in the air. He dribbled to the left, then to the right.

"Swing it!" his coach shouted from the sideline.

The clock was down to three. As he searched for an open man, he took his eyes off me. Here was my chance.

I swatted the ball from his hands and made a fast break for the basket. The crowd erupted! I dribbled to the hoop and shot.

Based on the cheering that echoed through the gym and the way the team lifted me up in joy, I figured I'd made the basket.

CHAPTER TWO

"Make way for the future of Granger hoops!" Marcus shouted as we walked together into Will Thompson's (much-too-large-to-be-legal) house. Marcus had convinced my mom that I had to come party. He gave her his solemn vow that he would look out for me.

My mom told Marcus that I could go under a few conditions: I had to be home by midnight. I couldn't drink anything except water or soda. And I couldn't get "fresh" with any young ladies. This made Marcus laugh out loud. Sean and I followed Marcus's lead as he walked over to Will Thompson III, who stood by a cooler of beers. Will was a post-grad senior and a strong defender, but he relied too much on his jump shot, which most of the time clanked off the rim. He was a legacy kid: both his father and his grandfather had attended Granger. His family made huge donations to the school, which translated to Will's getting lots of playing time, even when he didn't necessarily deserve it. All that playtime still hadn't gotten him recruited to Trinity College, so he was gracing the Granger School with another year of his presence and his parties.

Will was tall and lanky but had terrible posture, so to me he always looked like a question mark with floppy dirty-blond hair and thick eyebrows. By contrast, everything about Marcus screamed superstar in the making, from his red Jordans, gray jeans, and leather jacket to his all-AP class schedule to his talent on the court. I'd have been annoyed with him if he weren't so nice.

"Marcus! What up, playa?" Will asked, peering at us through oversized clown sunglasses.

Marcus and I looked at each other. I was silently asking if this guy was serious. Marcus had a look of resignation that said yes, indeed he was.

"Need a drink?" Will asked as he tossed me a can of Natty Light. Will was wearing an unofficial Granger Gunners T-shirt. Underneath the Gunners logo it read HERE TO STAY.

We'd been relegated to the basement, which was bigger than my home, a two-bedroom condo in Somerville. I didn't know what Will's family had done to amass this kind of wealth, but I knew the dude could afford more than Natty Light.

"Thanks," I said. I held the can, knowing full well I

wasn't going to open it. I would put it back in the cooler later. My mom wouldn't let me out of the house ever again if she smelled beer on my breath when I got home.

"That was a *nice* game you played, man. I didn't know you had it like that," Will said to me. He put on this Riff Raff–style accent he didn't have at school. I guess he spoke like that to anyone with more melanin than him, which included Marcus, Sean, and me.

This is the part where I'm supposed to use food metaphors to describe everyone's respective complexions. It makes me cringe a little, the way all the books we read in English class describe people's skin color using food metaphors. One day, when we were reading yet another description of a character with skin the color of caramel or chocolate, Elle pointed out that people aren't edible. I'd been thinking a lot about that. I thought about most things Elle said. Then I felt guilty when those thoughts spiraled to the two of us making out.

In food terms, I'd have deep olive skin, which I don't get, because aren't olives green? Anyway, Will is white, Marcus and Elle are black, and I am brown.

My mom, who is of Persian descent, was born and raised in the States. My dad grew up in Jordan and met my mom in Boston. He was Arab and had really light skin, and my mom is on the darker side. I came out somewhere in between.

"Your house is amazing," I told Will.

Sean stole the beer out of my hand. He flicked open the tab and took a swig. "Ahhh, that's fresh," he said, as if he drank beer all the time. The faker. His moms would be so disappointed.

"Oh, this old pile of bricks." Will said. "I can't complain, man. I'm blessed." It was almost like everything that came out of his mouth was something he'd rehearsed in a bathroom mirror. "You peeping on any bitches here tonight?"

I looked at Marcus as he pinched the bridge of his nose before turning away for a second. I couldn't tell if he was stopping himself from laughing in Will's face or if he was annoyed beyond belief.

"No worries," Will continued. "I got you. We got some fine chicks here tonight. You feel me?" He put his fist in the air, ready to be bumped.

I tapped it lightly with mine. I didn't want to be rude.

"Thanks. We'll go *peep*," Sean said, never one to sugarcoat his displeasure at the hypocrisies of high school nonsense.

"How about we say hey to some of your new fans, Beej," Marcus said, nodding in the direction of the New Crew, the most popular girls in the junior class.

"I don't know if I'd know what to say to El—to the group," I said. I could feel my face getting hot. "Are they fans? Really?"

"Marcus, may I have a word with your teammate?" Sean asked, scratching the back of his head.

"I'll see you two over there. Remember, I promised your mom: no getting fresh." Marcus wagged his finger at me before he walked over to Elle, Erin, and Jessica.

Sean put his hands on my shoulders, ready to deliver a patented inspirational speech. "Are you seriously not going to take this opportunity to talk to beautiful women?" he asked.

Sean and I have a lot in common—we love graphic novels, Stephen King, the Celtics; we both have jet-black hair; neither of us has a dad—but we differ in some ways too. He's half Japanese and half Irish, he's almost always in the ceramics room at school, and he's had sex. He doesn't lord it over me, which is nice. If the tables were turned, I would bring it up *all* the time. Sean never acts like he's superior to me because of his carnal knowledge, except when a group of pretty girls is standing nearby. Then he's the authority on talking to the ladies, though that night I didn't see him walking over to the New Crew on his own.

"Let me tell you something, Beej. Tonight is your night! You won Granger the game. We know athletics are the only thing people care about. Is that depressing? Sure! But you're a beneficiary now! Your mom raised you to be an upstanding young chap, you're smart, you're tall, and you can put together a mean bowl of cereal. You're a catch! Now we're going to go over there, and we're going to talk to those girls and impress them with some witty repartee, because the alternative is talking to ass hats like Will. You got it?"

"Can you imagine wearing an ass for a hat, though?" I asked in a weak attempt to kill my nerves.

"It's all I think about," Sean deadpanned. "You're deflecting. I appreciate that, but now is the time to step up, yes?"

"Yeah. Yeah, I got it."

"That's my guy. And break!" Sean slapped my shoulders as though we were leaving a huddle, but I didn't move.

The New Crew was standing with Marcus, hanging on his every word. To be fair, I sort of felt the same way when I talked to him. Elle and Jessica flanked their fearless flaxen-haired leader, Erin Wheeler, who wore a tight jean jacket over a skimpy black shirt. The three gorgeous young ladies were on yearbook staff. Some seniors had started calling them the New Crew when Erin and her friends were sophomores, and the name had stuck. They were to "run" the social scene once the senior yearbook girls graduated, though seniors cared less about the social hierarchy the closer they got to graduation. Drew Young, Erin's boyfriend, was there too. They were the "It" couple of our grade.

"Are you sure you want to go over there?" I asked Sean.

"Now or never," said Sean.

"How about never," I said, but Sean had already gripped my T-shirt and was tugging me toward them.

"Hey, guys," Marcus said, opening the circle to admit Sean and me. When Drew saw me coming, he made a break for the booze.

"Hey," Erin said, acknowledging us momentarily before checking her phone.

I'd never gotten a read on Erin over the years. She'd never been mean to me specifically, but there was a frostiness to her. The rumor was that she'd have to be held back a year if she didn't get her grades up, but so far she was managing to stay in our class.

"Hi, Bijan," Elle said. My heart felt like the Grinch's, expanding three sizes with Elle's voice evoking all the Whos in Who-ville singing on Christmas Day. "You played really well tonight."

Once, I managed to start a conversation with Elle at a sophomore dance. I said "Hi, Elle." When she said hi back, I froze. I hadn't planned for her to say hi back! I smiled a lot, and then, when I couldn't form any more words, she politely excused herself to get some punch.

Did I put Elle on a pedestal? Yes. Did she have reason to be on that pedestal? Absolutely. She was brilliant, kind, and stunning. She nibbled on her pencil erasers during English class, which was so cute . . . not that I looked at her all the time! Mostly I said "hey" to her during English class, which was a step up from "Derrrrrr . . . uhhhhh . . . you're soooooooo pretty." I'd never said that out loud, but I'd been tempted to.

"Bijan Majidi is not one to choke under pressure, yet he seems to be faltering now, Reggie."

"He had better start saying something soon, Kevin, or she is going to think he is super creepy."

"Hi, Elle. You too."

"Did he just say 'you too,' as though she played in the game?"

"He sure did, Kevin. He sure did."

Her high cheekbones and long eyelashes were making me incoherent. "Sorry. I mean, uh, thank you. W-we all played well, so . . ." I stammered as my face grew hot. I caught Jessica looking at me with surprise and heard Sean clear his throat. My face must have been burning like an animated case of athlete's foot in a Lotrimin commercial. Elle didn't say anything, but she was smiling.

"Not a bad recovery . . . Maybe she didn't notice?"

"Are you serious, Kevin?"

"But enough about us," said Marcus, saving me from embarrassing myself further. "What's going on for the rest of tonight?"

"Well, Drew's probably going to pass out soon," Erin said, watching Drew chug down something in a red Solo cup while other guys from the team cheered him on. "So I guess not much." For the life of me, I will never understand what girls see in Drew Young.

Erin's phone buzzed again. She let out an exasperated sigh at her screen and shoved the phone into her jeans pocket. "Yeah, I'm not looking forward to driving him home later."

"You could leave him here," Sean said with a shrug before taking another swig.

"That's not a bad idea, actually," Erin said. Beer frothed down Drew's chin while he high-fived his whooping buddies. Will and his pals joined in, jumping and yelling.

"Excuse me a moment," Marcus said as he walked over to his teammates. This left Sean and me alone.

Alone.

With.

The.

Girls.

I was not prepared.

"All this party is missing is a piñata full of hundred-dollar bills, right?" I asked with a little chuckle that quickly turned into a whimper because Jessica was staring at me like I had just expressed my undying affection for jockstraps. "Is there any food, or is that not a thing at this kind of party?"

"That would be a *fun* party," Elle responded. "Unlike this one. I was kind of hoping to have a girls' night with my friends at home." She said the last bit while looking at Jessica.

"I couldn't not come to his party," Jessica said. "I'm his girlfriend."

"When it's convenient for him," Elle grumbled. "He hasn't said much to you or your friends all night."

"You can do better," Erin chimed in.

"Maybe some of us aren't as picky as you, Elle," Jessica said, ignoring Erin. "It's high school and he's hot. Enough said." Jessica's freckled face became a little pink.

"Will is pretty handsome. For a Neanderthal," Sean interjected.

"Sorry . . . Remind me, why are you here?" Jessica asked.

"I'm here as Bijan's moral support," Sean said. "Plus beer. Moral support and beer."

Jessica put her focus back on me, ignoring Sean.

"So, are you, like, on varsity now?" Jessica showed off her toothy grin. "Will didn't mention you were going to play."

"It was a last-minute thing. Kevin was pretty badly injured last game, so Coach Johnson asked me to fill in," I said.

"I was just asking because we already took the team photo for yearbook," Jessica said. "But we can totally add a separate photo of you."

"Yeah, like an action shot of him scoring the winning hoop tonight," Sean said, slapping me on the back.

"How is the yearbook coming along?" I asked Elle. Opportunities to talk to her at a cool-kid party didn't come very often. Now that I was here, I wanted to make the most of it.

"Well, it's—" Elle began.

"It's so much work, but it's *so* rewarding," Jessica answered, cutting Elle off.

"Sorry, I was asking Elle," I said. Jessica wasn't grinning anymore. She took a sip from her drink and glowered at me over the rim of her cup.

"No way," Erin said, looking behind me, as her face turned a shade of pepperoni.

I turned my head to find Stephanie Bergner and Noah Olson walking down the stairs. People usually rolled their eyes whenever Stephanie spoke, and a lot of guys called her Busted Bergner, but she was okay. She was a little intense, but it was kind of cool how she was involved in *everything*. She was in the finance club and on the debate team, and she was my grade's student council representative. She also played the cello in orchestra and at all the school talent shows. The cello didn't exactly get the crowd going, but she was good at it. I liked the way her face scrunched up when she played.

Stephanie, all five foot two inches of her, still in her school uniform and penny loafers, marched over to us. A pink headband held her wavy light brown hair in place.

"Fellow juniors! Nice to have solidarity in numbers," Stephanie said as though she were campaigning for next year's student council election. Noah lingered behind her. He gave me a bro nod.

Noah was pleasant most of the time. We had been lab partners in chemistry sophomore year. He was reliable and did his work, but he always felt the need to look over my answers before handing them in with his, which bothered me. I got better grades on our tests, but he was sure he was smarter than me.

"What are you guys doing here?" Elle asked. Her tone wasn't malicious. I think, like the rest of us, she was surprised that Stephanie had decided to be social.

"Yes, why are we here?" Noah asked. He seemed annoyed to be at the big party of the weekend and not alone with Stephanie. He was wearing "date night" clothes: chinos and a tucked-in Ralph Lauren button-down. His hair was slicked back with gel.

"She's here for the same reason we all are. To have a great time," Sean deadpanned before letting out an unapologetic burp. Mama Hana would have been disgusted. Mom Jane would have been pleased that Sean was trying, in his own way, to make a newcomer feel welcome.

"I got a text that there would be a party this evening," Stephanie explained. Erin's green eyes widened, as if she was shocked anyone would invite Stephanie Bergner to a Thompson house party. "I thought it might be good to get some signatures while people are in a compliant state."

Noah, as if on cue, passed her a clipboard. He seemed to be enthusiastic about causes, but only when Stephanie was involved. I'd never seen him take on a community project on his own.

"What's the petition for this time?" Jessica asked. "Not enough kale in the cafeteria?"

"I am willing to let that little jab slide. It would be wonderful if you would participate in our mascot change campaign, Jessica."

"You can't let that go, can you?" Erin asked. At the end of last year, Stephanie had written a guest opinion piece for our school paper, the *Granger Gazette*. In it, she'd said that our mascot, the Gunner, was inappropriate for a school environment. Initially, it hadn't struck a chord. For the most part, we all kind of went about our day-to-day lives and got ready for summer vacation.

That was until Will Thompson's grandfather, who was a member of the school's board of trustees as well as an esteemed donor, got wind of the article. He wrote his own op-ed for Granger's glossy alumni magazine, discussing his disappointment with the lack of respect for tradition.

Mr. Thompson's piece galvanized Stephanie's cause, and suddenly a group of students and their parents began to voice their opinions online and in person at school events. I'd thought discussion would die down over the summer, but Stephanie and a sizable group of students hadn't forgotten about it when they showed up at this fall's homecoming game. She and Noah had made T-shirts. On the front was a graphic of the Gunners rifle crossed out Ghostbusters-style. NO TRADITION OF VIOLENCE was written on the back. Fifty or so students lined up on the sidelines along with Stephanie, wearing the shirts. Nobody booed them. People noticed and gave them dirty looks, but the only booing during the game was when the refs made calls in favor of Armstead Academy's team.

"The petition is to change the Granger School's mascot from the Gunners to something nonviolent but still in line with the school's history," Stephanie said. She blinked an awful lot. It must have been stressful, being that smart around people who didn't appreciate it.

"We're hoping to work with the administration on choosing a more inclusive mascot," Noah explained. "As soon as we have enough signatures, we can make a motion to meet with the board of trustees."

"I like the mascot the way it is," Jessica said. Stephanie wasn't going to have much luck with this crowd.

"You have a right to your opinion, however backward it may be," Stephanie replied. Elle laughed, and Erin smiled a little before she remembered she wasn't supposed to be amused by anything Stephanie Bergner said. Her face reset to ambivalent frostiness, but Jessica had already noticed. She nudged Erin with her elbow.

"I don't think this is the time or place for a petition," Erin said. Stephanie squared up to Erin, her penny loafers toe-to-toe with Erin's Frye boots. Erin stared right back at her, like she was trying to figure out which planet Stephanie came from. Were they going to have a catfight?

"You weren't invited tonight," Erin said coolly. Stephanie's face crumpled. I knew I shouldn't get involved, but I had never seen Stephanie Bergner cry. I didn't plan to if I could help it. We nerds had to stick together.

"I invited her," I lied.

"You what?" Erin and Noah asked me in unison.

Everybody stared. I couldn't be sure, but Elle might have smiled a little. Maybe that was wishful thinking.

"You invited her?" Erin asked. She was giving me a kind of evil squint. I wondered if *we* were going to fight. I wouldn't last a round of that battle.

"Yeah, I texted her after the big win. Wanted my buddy here to celebrate." I grinned at her. Stephanie stood up straight, her chest puffed out like Andre Iguodala's after he scored a three-pointer. "Should we get some people to sign?" I asked, offering my elbow to her like dudes do to women in old movies.

"I would be amenable to that. Thank you," Stephanie said, linking her arm with mine. We moseyed over to the other side of the room, where some of the boys' varsity ice hockey team members were playing beer pong. Three of them were wearing the same HERE TO STAY shirt Will had on. I had a feeling they wouldn't be signing Stephanie's petition.

Her arm felt good linked with mine, and it sucked when she pulled away. It would be so great to walk around like that with a girl all the time. Well, not all the time—I'd have to unlink to go to the bathroom—but it'd be awesome to walk with someone who was as proud of me as I was of her.

"Thanks for saying that," Stephanie said as she adjusted her headband, making sure her long brown hair was tucked behind her ears.

"No sweat! Next time I win the social lottery prize, I'll invite you for real," I said.

"I meant the buddy portion. I don't have that many *buddies* at present, aside from Noah. I saw the game. You were very good."

"Thanks! I guess I played well enough to get invited to one of these things. Are we supposed to be having fun now?"

"We'd probably have a better time if we were drinking. Only I find the notion of not being in control of myself a little unnerving," Stephanie said, looking over her shoulder at Jessica, Elle, and Erin.

"Well, that's a better reason than being terrified of your mom," I said. "If my mom smells me reeking of booze, she'll lock me up in my room until the dystopian future arrives. That is, if we aren't living in one now."

"I'm fairly certain we are," Stephanie said, taking in the landscape of girls snapping selfies and dudes shotgunning beers, foamy suds spilling onto the light green carpeting. Sean was shotgunning. I knew I shouldn't have left him alone with seniors. "Shall we ask your teammates for some signatures?"

"Oh, well, they're not exactly my teammates. I mean, I'm just on loan from JV," I said, but she kept walking. She was on a mission.

"Gentlemen, good evening, and well done on a great game," she said as she approached them.

"Busted Bergner! What's good?" a rosy-cheeked, droopy-eyed Drew Young asked. Stephanie flinched a little. I'm sure she was aware of the nickname, but that was different from hearing someone say it to her face.

"Always a pleasure to see you, Drew," Stephanie said dryly. "We were wondering if you would be interested in signing a petition to change the school's mascot to something less violent but still formidable?"

Drew looked at her clipboard as he took a long swig from his cup. Then he looked up at me. He seemed more annoyed with me than he did with Stephanie. He slapped his heavy hand on the back of my neck.

"Hey, man, come celebrate with us and quit wasting time with her," Drew slurred, slamming a can of beer against my chest. That would leave a bruise.

"Thanks," I said as I clutched the can. Drew's breath smelled like cold cuts that had been left in the sun too long.

"Go ahead. Drink it," Drew said. His eyelids fluttered. He wobbled a little too.

"I think you've had enough for the both of us, man." I patted his shoulder. He jerked away from me.

"Drink the beer. It's just a Natty Light. Allah's not gonna mind." His smirk was suddenly not so playful. "If you don't want my beer, it's cool. I mean, it's weird, but it's fine," Drew said. "You played one good game. One. So what? I bust my ass every game and at every practice."

"I used to have my fair share of dealing with trash talkers, Kevin. You gotta give what you get! John Starks learned that the hard way in the 1995 playoffs. You remember that series?"

"Not the time to reminisce, Reggie. Not the time."

"You're right. It was just one game. For now," I said, trying to defuse the situation—though maybe I straightened my posture a bit to let him know I was not one to mess with. At six foot four, I've got inches on Drew, but he's more built than I am. I'm lean and he's stocky. He has the body of a non-steroid-using wrestler.

"You got lucky. That's all," he said as his head lolled forward and he stumbled even closer to me.

"There's no need for conflict," Stephanie said. She squirmed her way between us.

"Oh! Intercepted by Bergner! Having a girl come to the rescue, that must be a blow."

"How's your sister Cheryl, by the way? Didn't she earn way more accolades than you growing up?"

"Point taken, Kevin."

"Stephanie, it's okay. I got it," I whispered.

"I took a seminar on conflict resolution at Emerson last summer. I'd like to put what I learned into practice," she whispered back, then turned. "Now, Drew, I can understand that you've been drinking, but why don't we all take a deep breath—" Drew leaned forward and spewed chunks all over her penny loafers.

"*Oh, technical foul! Are you kidding me? Somebody eject this guy!*"

"*Looks like Drew Young really enjoyed the beef stew at the cafeteria today, Reggie.*"

I pulled Stephanie back by her sweater, doing my best to keep her away from the exodus of booze, Gatorade, and nastiness coming out of Drew's mouth.

"I think I'd like to go home now," Stephanie squealed as she stepped out of her soggy shoes. The party, for Stephanie and me, was over. We weren't really supposed to be there anyway.

CHAPTER THREE

It was seven a.m. on Sunday when my phone buzzed and fell off my bedside table. It vibrated on the floor until I got out of bed to see who would call me at such an insane hour. I didn't recognize the number. If it was a scammer posing as an employee of the IRS, I was going to be pissed.

"Hello?" I said, answering.

"Good morning! This is Stephanie. Bergner. You assisted me at Will Thompson's party?"

"Oh. Hi," I slurred, half conscious. How had she gotten my number? Why couldn't she text, like everybody else?

"I wanted to thank you for your kindness. Noah was a bit squeamish at the sight of my vomit-soaked shoes, but you weren't, which I found to be quite admirable. So thank you," she said.

"No problem," I said before I yawned loudly.

"I've called you at a bad time, haven't I? I forget not everyone is a morning person," she said.

"Izzz okay," I managed, rubbing sleep boogers from my eyes.

"Oh, good! Since I have you on the phone, I was wondering if you would be interested in helping get signatures for our mascot petition tomorrow at lunch?"

"What? Oh, I don't know," I said as the sleepy fog began to clear.

"Noah, Elle, and I will be at a table in the cafeteria. It's fairly informal. We'll be asking students and teachers passing by if they'd like to sign."

"Elle's going to do it?" I asked, my eyes widening at the mention of her name.

"Yes! I think her involvement will really get some of the more popular students to participate. By 'popular,' I mean those students that fit a construct of what high school-aged peers deem to be cool. Though my father says those things don't matter in college. I can't wait for college." Stephanie talked so fast I couldn't tell if she was actually breathing.

"Yeah, okay. I'll join, I guess," I muttered, lying back down on my bed.

"Wonderful! I think this will really help us keep the momentum going," she said. "Now, I think what we might consider doing is sending out an email blast and then—"

"Okay. Bye," I said as I hung up on her midsentence. It was rude, but so was waking up a guy on a Sunday morning.

* * *

"Since when do you care about the school mascot?" Sean asked me as we walked to the cafeteria from the schoolhouse that Monday. He didn't wear a coat over his uniform like I did as we trudged out into the cold. When I first started at Granger, it was a little overwhelming to travel around the five-hundred-acre campus full of giant Gregorian buildings like I was already at college. Sometimes I took for granted how good I had it, being part of a place that made you feel like you were on the verge of greatness.

"I see what Stephanie's saying. It's kind of messed up to have a guy carrying a rifle as a mascot for a school," I said.

"Yeah, but why not get involved last year? Or you could sign the thing and be done with it?"

I opened the heavy wooden door leading to the dining hall. When Sean saw Elle behind a long folding table, collecting signatures with Stephanie and Noah, he busted out laughing.

"What did James Brown used to sing, Kevin? I know you're old enough to remember. 'This is a man's world, but it wouldn't be nothing without a woman or a girl'?"

"I personally liked his ditty 'Living in America' from Rocky IV.*"*

"The one where Rocky single-handedly ended the Cold War?"

"Ha! Well, yes, I suppose he did, Reggie. I suppose he did. God, I miss the eighties."

"Bijan! Sean! Hello!" Stephanie said. Two sophomores signed the clipboard in front of Elle. Stephanie was right: Elle's presence gave the campaign much-needed star quality.

"Glad to have your support, Beej!" Noah's smile was a little too earnest. I wasn't thrilled that he called me Beej. Sean and Marcus could, but from Noah, it felt forced.

"Happy to help. So long as we don't get a mascot like G-Wiz," I joked, unzipping my coat. Stephanie, Elle, and Noah didn't react, so naturally I couldn't help myself. I let the useless NBA trivia fly. "G-Wiz. He's this weird blue alien thing for the Washington Wizards. He looks like Cookie Monster on drugs."

"I know to which mascot you were referring," Stephanie said. "Do you assume I don't know about sports because I am female identified?"

"BANG! He did not see that one coming, Reggie!"

"No! I just . . . you, um . . . I think women are great! So great!" I hesitated when I saw Elle raise her eyebrows. She either found me entertaining or couldn't believe I was rambling the way I was. Noah smirked. I was on my own. I really did not like that he'd called me Beej.

"To be fair, I don't watch the NBA, but I did do my homework on mascots," Stephanie said with a hint of a grin. "I'm more of a soccer fan. Have a seat next to Elle, please."

"Yeah, Beej. Have a seat next to Elle," Sean said. I could feel my ears burn as I sat down. I took off my coat, but it didn't do much to cool me down. Sean signed the clipboard in front of Elle and me before he went to grab food.

"Hello again," Elle said.

"Hi." In my head I went through things I could say to impress her. *You come to this cafeteria often? How'd you get so perfect? If you had to pick, which would you prefer, muffins for hands or pickles for toes?* "Have you had much luck getting signatures yet?"

"Not really. It's kind of disappointing, but I'm late to the Great Mascot Debate," Elle said. "Thanks for doing this. I tried to convince my friends, but they said it's a waste of time."

"It's no big thing." I somehow managed to make eye contact. Her curly hair was in a half ponytail. When she looked at me with her big brown eyes, the inside of my chest felt like it was made of warm, gooey burnt marshmallows from campfire s'mores.

"Majidi has to stop staring at her before it gets creepy, Reggie."

"Young fella hears you loud and clear. He is going to remember to blink and look away every so often."

"How was the rest of the party?" I asked her, trying to play it cool.

"Erin and I left shortly after you did. Jessica stayed behind to argue with her on-again, off-again man-baby." She scowled. "Sorry. I don't know if Will's your friend."

"I don't know him personally," I answered. "But I'd like to think you and I are friends, so if you say he's a man-baby, then he's a man-baby."

"Did Majidi just friend-zone himself?"

"Better to be in the friend zone than not in the game at all, Reggie. Let's see if big fella can hang in there."

"I loved your photo exhibit at last semester's Arts Night," I said, trying to change the subject. Sean had wanted to scope out the showcase to get an idea for his own show this semester, and I'd tagged along. "The picture of your grandmother on the beach was my favorite."

"Oh, thank you," she said. Her eyes lit up in surprise. "I didn't know you were there." She shook her head. "Sorry, that was rude. I mean, it was crowded, and I was so nervous to show my stuff—"

"It's okay! I kind of blend in, in a crowd, especially here," I joked. The hallowed halls of Granger had more kids who looked like Erin and Will walking in them than kids who looked like me or Elle. "Well, maybe I don't blend in per se, but my photo is usually used in the admissions brochures," I said. "So people are used to seeing me."

"You too? Gee, I wonder why," she said with a sigh. "They put a picture of me and Erin in our squash uniforms on the school's home page."

"That's because you two are so photogenic." I paused a moment, realizing I maybe shouldn't have said that. "There's a photo of me in the admissions packet looking through a microscope. We weren't even using the microscopes that day in lab, but the photographer guy asked me to look into it," I said, rolling my eyes. "Anyway, I loved your exhibition."

"Thank you. It took a while to get the photo the way I wanted it. My grandmother kept posing for a glamour shot. I had to explain that I wanted her to look more natural."

"Well, I thought it was great. She must have been very proud of you."

"They're locking eyes!"

"Majidi is trying to connect. . . ."

"Hey, Beej," Marcus said as he walked up to our table. "I didn't know you were a part of this whole thing."

"Oh! Time-out called by Marcus Silva. You hate to see that, Reggie."

"I'm, uh, helping out today," I said, fidgeting in my chair. I could feel Elle shift in her seat too.

"What are you going to change the mascot to, exactly?" Marcus asked Stephanie. He leaned over and bumped my fist.

"That is yet to be determined," Stephanie said. "Ideally, the student body will be involved in choosing something nonviolent and culturally sensitive."

Marcus nodded and then picked up the pen and signed. "I hope you'll want my input when the time comes. No Bobcats. I feel like everyone is a Bobcat these days," he said before he walked away.

"That's a big-time name on the list," I said to the table as I pointed to Marcus's signature. "I mean, when guys see his name on the page, I'm sure they'll sign on."

Stephanie was beaming, but Elle didn't look so convinced. She was more in tune with Marcus's social circle than I was.

* * *

As lunch went on, we got eleven more signatures. Most people didn't even bother looking at our table. My history teacher, Ms. McCrea, came over to sign, but the teachers who walked in with her booked it to the lunch trays. Either they were in a rush or they were very aware that private-school teachers couldn't get tenure and didn't want to rock the boat over a mascot.

"I really admire all of you for sticking with this," Ms. McCrea said. She was wearing a floral-print skirt that went all the way to the ground. I worried she might trip on it, but she never did.

Ms. McCrea was a pretty decent history teacher, as well as the dean of students, but if you wanted to kill time in class, all you had to do was ask her about her year volunteering abroad after college. She'd eat up the whole class talking about her experience in Bolivia like she was the only American to ever visit there. Sean was always the biggest perpetrator of said strategy, especially on days when he had a quiz in another class and wanted to slyly check his index cards while she prattled on.

"Bijan, you had a tremendous game on Friday! I had no idea you played," Ms. McCrea said. I suppose she didn't catch many JV games.

"Thanks," I said.

"Yes, we're excited to have an athlete step up for the cause," Noah said. He didn't sound excited. He sounded irritated. "Hopefully his participation will influence some of his fellow student athletes. Right, Stephanie?"

"Translation: Why else would you have this jock help us? At least, that's the vibe I'm picking up, Kevin."

"Ms. McCrea says her goodbyes, and we're back to the starting lineup. It's been a pretty slow lunch, and the shot clock is ticking."

Erin, Drew, Will, and Jessica strolled into the cafeteria. Will's arm was draped over Jessica's shoulder, so I guess they were on again. Drew was holding hands with Erin, but she let go of him and walked up to Elle.

"How's it going?" Erin looked at the half-empty paper in front of us.

"You guys got nothing else to do?" Will asked.

"It was either this or listen to you talk about your stats

from last week's game again," Elle said, placing her chin in her hand. Jessica winced.

"You love it," Will said with a laugh. Then he turned to me. "How'd you get roped into this?"

I wasn't sure how to answer him. The truth was, I didn't really care either way what the mascot was, but I couldn't say that with Elle sitting next to me and not sound like an insensitive jerk.

"It'd be cool to change things up. Maybe have a lion or a grizzly on the uniform," I said, spreading my hand across my chest. "As long as the animal isn't packing, of course."

"How much would that cost?" Drew asked. "To change everything?"

I looked at Stephanie for an answer, but she only blinked at him. I think she was as shocked as I was that she didn't have a response.

"We, uh, haven't gotten to that in our proposal yet," Noah mumbled.

"I see," Drew said. "So you haven't gotten an estimate for what a new paint job would cost for the gym, the hallways, the ice hockey rink? You haven't thought about how much it might cost to buy new uniforms for all the sports teams, change all the school's merchandise, how much the school would have to spring for a new PR campaign instead of spending that money on teachers or financial aid? What do you think that'd do for the school's costs? Maybe hike tuition a bit?"

"We could have a bake sale?" Noah offered.

Drew's jaw clenched and his brow furrowed. "Sorry about your shoes," he said to Stephanie before he walked off.

Will let go of Jessica's shoulder. "I'm so hungry, babe," he declared. "You can stay or whatever, but I'm starving. See you later." He jogged off too. Jessica huffed as she watched him go and then turned to direct her ire at those of us at the table.

"I don't get *why* you want to change the mascot," Jessica said to Elle.

"I'm not crazy about wearing a colonial soldier carrying a gun on my jersey every time I go to a match," Elle said.

"Don't you like the sense of tradition?" Jessica responded. "It's commemorating those who fought in the Revolutionary War."

"The Granger School wasn't even around during the Revolutionary War," Elle said. "Plus, what does war have to do with my education?"

"If we sign it, will you come grab lunch with us?" Erin was asking Elle, but she was staring down Stephanie.

"Lunch is almost over. I don't see why not," Stephanie said, meeting Erin's eyes. It looked like they were about to fight again, but Erin broke the staring contest and signed the clipboard in front of Stephanie. She sauntered into the dining hall, with Jessica following her.

"I'll see you all later. Let me know how else I can help,"

Elle said to Stephanie as she stood. Then there were three of us.

"It's all right if you want to go too," Noah told me. He obviously wanted to be alone with Stephanie.

"Hey, I'm happy to stay on as long as you need," I said.

Before Stephanie could respond, Coach Johnson approached our table. He was wearing his classroom outfit: slacks with a button-down shirt and tie. He kind of reminded me of Coach Gregg Popovich of the San Antonio Spurs, but with a little more meat around his midsection and in his face. "Just the man I was looking for," he said to me. "I got something to talk to you about."

"Coach Johnson, will you sign our petition?" Stephanie asked. Coach looked at the clipboard briefly, then backed away, shaking his head. "Maybe some other time. Mind if I borrow B for a minute?"

"By all means," Stephanie said politely. I got up and followed Coach over to the end of the faculty lunch table, where he gestured for me to sit across from him. Ms. McCrea sat at the end with other teachers and waved at me.

"How you doing, son? Did you get anything to eat?"

"Uh, no, I was going to grab a bagel or something." It wasn't lost on me that he still hadn't said my name.

"I'll write you a note for your next class so you can get something more substantial," Coach said. "That was a hell of a game you played for us on Friday."

"Thanks. It was really great to be out there."

"Do you think you could play like that for the rest of the season? As an official member of the varsity squad?"

"For real? Well, yeah, I'd love to! I mean, if it's okay with Coach Matthews." I didn't want to leave Sean and the rest of JV team high and dry.

"Ah, their season's pretty much done anyway. We need you for these next two weeks. It's playoff time, and, well, I don't need to tell you this, but with Donaldson out, you've seen how the team isn't quite itself right now."

"Yeah, I'd love to play! Thanks."

Coach Johnson extended his hand for me to shake. "Glad to hear it. You play like you did on Friday and we should be all set to win the New England tourney." His grip tightened. "But you've got to listen to me on the court. You can't make stuff up as you go, like with that last play on Friday. Understand?"

"Yeah, sure thing, Coach," I said. He released my hand. He took out a pad of paper and pen to write me a note so I could show up late to next period.

"We're going to need you to focus. Best not to waste your time on any political movements or whatever is going on over there," he said, nodding in Stephanie's direction. "How do you spell your last name, again?"

"M-A-J-I-D-I."

"That an Irish name?" He handed me the slip with a laugh. "Shouldn't be too hard to fit that on a varsity jacket. Welcome to the team, kid. See you at practice this afternoon."

He stood up and patted me on the shoulder before he left the cafeteria. I wasn't so hungry anymore.

CHAPTER FOUR

"All right, choose your guys," Coach Johnson ordered as he tugged at his belt buckle. We'd been through the new plays and done our layup drills. Now Coach had decided to have us scrimmage, shirts versus skins.

As varsity cocaptains, Marcus and Todd were in charge of choosing teams. Marcus, team shirt, had first pick. Before he even said anything, Drew took a step forward.

"Beej," Marcus said, pointing at me.

"Present?" I said. Had he called *me* before Drew?

"Let's go." Marcus waved me over. I jogged to half-court, then turned to face the rest of the team. Drew's look of confusion quickly dissolved into a scowl. Will, who stood next to him, whispered something in his ear. Whatever he said didn't help Drew's mood.

"Drew," Todd called. Drew stared daggers at me as he

walked over. He took off his shirt and tossed it to the sidelines. Some girls from the varsity squash team catcalled as they ran on the track above us. I hoped Elle wasn't one of them, because if Drew was the kind of guy she liked, I needed to hit the free weights. Dude was jacked, all sinewy. He had muscles I wasn't sure human beings were supposed to have. The rest of the lineup was assembled with no surprises.

My team started with the ball. Drew didn't even bother to guard me. He gave me lots of space around the arc. Marcus threw me a hard chest pass. I made a shot so pretty that he clapped his hands before we ran back on defense.

"And . . . BANG! He gets the three!"

"What makes Majidi so dynamic is his ability to make three-point shots when Granger needs him to."

"Good thing he had lots of practice shooting by himself on weekends, Kevin. Who needs a girlfriend when you've got basketball?"

"Nice shot, Beej!" Marcus bellowed.

"Will Thompson inbounds to Drew Young, who brings the ball downcourt. Our young buck Majidi is all over him like Gold Bond on Shaq's chest!"

"But not to be undone, Drew whips it over to Towering Todd for an easy layup."

"It looks like it's the battle of the shooting guards, Kev!"

I followed Drew until a ton of bricks slammed into my shoulder and I spilled onto the floor. The whistle blew. Will leaned over me, grinning, obviously pleased with his work.

"You got to be prepared for anything, newbie," Will said.

"That kind of crap isn't going to fly come game time, Thompson," Coach yelled.

Will shrugged. "Just toughening him up."

The skins scored. I pushed myself up and inbounded the ball to Marcus. He looked down the floor to map out his options—until Drew decided to guard him, that is. Watching them play one-on-one was like watching two dance partners perform their greatest hits. The rest of us on the court stopped running around. This was personal. They knew each other's every move, every intention; knew every reason why they played.

But Marcus wasn't giving the ball to anyone. He tripped Drew up with a nasty crossover. Drew slipped and fell forward onto his knees.

"Marcus Silva is on a tear today!"

"I hope Drew Young has the phone number of a good orthopedist. He's going to need it if he keeps falling for Silva's ankle-breakers."

Marcus drove to the hoop for an easy layup and scooped up his own rebound. He passed to Drew with a nod.

Drew slammed the ball down in frustration.

"Young surges full steam ahead, trying to shake off that embarrassment as best he can."

"Embarrassment is right, Kevin. I mean . . . he fell for that crossover hook, line, and sinker."

"Majidi runs back to stay with him. Young stops at the top of the key. He buries a jump shot right in front of Majidi's face."

"Your boy can't guard me, Marcus!" Drew shouted so everyone in the gym could hear—including Elle, Erin, and the rest of the girls' varsity squash team, still running on the track above us.

I inbounded the ball to Marcus again. But he immediately passed it back. He wanted me to prove Drew wrong, to see what I would do when Marcus was no longer leading the team. Drew lunged at me, swatted the ball, and stole it away. I chased him down, running as fast as I could to make sure he didn't get a layup.

"Here comes Young, about to shoot . . . and BANG, Majidi is right there, slapping the rock away from behind!"

"Bijan is channeling Dikembe Mutombo! Letting Young know it is time to get out of his house!"

I blocked the hell out of that shot, and *everyone* knew it. My teammates laughed and cheered.

Drew turned around to look at me. He was inches away from my face. "That was a foul," he barked.

"It was all ball. You know it was," I said calmly.

"Bull," Drew said. He pushed his shoulder into mine as he walked past me. "Poser," he mumbled so only I could hear it.

"Don't be mad 'cause you can't play," I yelled.

"Nail him, Drew!" Will shouted from the other end of the court.

Drew turned around, his fists balled up as he rushed me. I braced myself, remembering what my mom had told me in elementary school: *If someone pushes you, you push them right back.* It didn't come to that. Coach Johnson blew his whistle.

"My office, you two! Now!" he shouted. He blew his whistle again to corral everyone else into the locker room. After that, the gym was eerily quiet. I looked up. The squash team had stopped running to watch. Elle looked down at me like a celestial being taking in the mortals and their foolish antics down below.

* * *

"What the hell am I supposed to do with you two?" Coach Johnson asked in an unsettlingly calm tone of voice. Drew and I sat in front of his desk as he paced back and forth behind it. His polo shirt with the Gunners logo in the top right corner had sweat stains under the armpits. "You know we're in elimination mode. One loss, we're done for the season. You think I care about your pissing contest? That kind of behavior out there? That makes you undesirable to a college campus," he said, momentarily standing still. "You know what *undesirable* is, gentlemen? It means you may have been getting scouted for a decent school. They look at what you accomplished here. Your test scores, your grades, whatever the hell it is you managed to do for yourself. And then you blow all that with some stupid disciplinary problems." Coach stared at Drew, who slumped in his chair. "When I scouted you for this place, you were all in." The red in Coach's neck rose to his face. "Now you're picking fights at practice. You think the school pays for you to come here so you can pull this crap?"

Drew was on financial aid? I knew he was about to fight me on the court, but now I kind of felt sorry for him. He slumped farther down in his seat and stared at the carpet. I don't know why Coach felt it was okay to talk to him like that in front of me. I guessed that was what happened when you made it to varsity. I wasn't into it.

Coach then aimed his rant at me, but I could see he was cooling down. "B, you're just starting out with us, and you've got a great future ahead of you. Why do you want to squander your big chance on pointless skirmishes?" I fought the urge to tell Coach that I hadn't started anything. I'd blocked Drew's shot and he didn't like it. Was I not supposed to play to the best of my ability?

"So here's a plan we can all agree to: say you're sorry, shake hands, and guarantee me there isn't going to be any more trouble from the two of you."

Drew reluctantly stuck his hand out to me. I shook it. Hard. Neither one of us apologized, but the handshake seemed to be enough for Coach. "Fine. Now, Drew, get out of my sight for today. B, you stay. I want to talk to you."

Drew looked slightly panicked that he was being dismissed when I wasn't. He gave me a long stare before he got out of his chair and left Coach Johnson's office. Coach sat behind his desk, taking a few deep breaths before he addressed me.

"With all due respect, he came at me, Coach," I said. Coach held up his hands like he had already had enough of me explaining myself.

"The guys don't know you well enough yet. You need time to gel with the team. Let them see what you can do."

Right, the game. Let's focus on the game, the important thing.

"All you have to do is keep your nose clean, do your thing on the court, you'll be golden. If any of the guys give you guff, come to me first, okay?"

I didn't know if I would want to go to him for anything. I'd have to trust him to do that. If he could say those things to Drew, what did he plan to say to me someday?

CHAPTER FIVE

I slogged up the plowed driveway from the gym, past the snow-dusted baseball field and the ice hockey rink to get to the schoolhouse. The sports complex, with its state-of-the-art facilities, was a more recent addition to the school, but it was kind of a trek on a cold day in February. Some lazy seniors would drive and wave at underclassmen on their way down. Even if I had a car, I don't think I'd do that. Well, maybe if I had a car, I'd do lots of other things instead of trying to catch the last bus.

I don't know why I was surprised to find out that Drew was on financial aid. I guess I assumed because he and Will hung out, they were both set up for life. My mom makes a good living, but I still need an academic scholarship to help with tuition. Besides, I was supposed to be mad at him, not worried about his dumb feelings.

I walked up to the main schoolhouse entrance to find Stephanie Bergner sitting on one of the benches outside. Her line of sight led straight to Drew, who was arguing with Erin a half-court bounce pass away. Will and Jessica stood near Stephanie, watching the fight as well. Will looked bemused. Jessica was biting her lower lip.

"Did the bus leave already?" I asked Stephanie as I sat down beside her.

"I don't know," Stephanie said. She kept her eye on the quarreling lovebirds. We had front-row seats.

"Do you want a ride or not, Drew?" Erin asked.

"I don't get why you felt the need to lie to me," Drew said as Erin pulled her car keys out of her coat pocket.

"I don't need to tell you where I'll be at all times, Drew." Erin was cool as Mr. Freeze explaining mastermind plots to Batman. Not the Arnold Schwarzenegger version of Mr. Freeze from *Batman & Robin*; I like to pretend that movie never existed. "So I stayed after school to study at the library. So what?"

"You straight up lied to my face today at lunch when I asked you if you were going to be around after practice. You said no, you were going home. Yet here you are, coming out of the library with Busted Bergner." Drew stabbed a finger in Stephanie's direction.

"The library was closing. I can't control when people decide to leave the building," Erin said, without taking her eyes off Drew.

"Be honest with me, okay? And don't be a bitch to me in front of my friends."

"Don't be a what?" Stephanie jumped up from her seat and marched toward the couple.

"Oh my God, it's the feminist police." Drew threw his hands in the air like Coach did when a player messed up.

"You're going to let him call you that?" Stephanie asked Erin, who ignored her and continued to focus on Drew. Stephanie looked like she wanted to shoot heat vision at Drew from eyes narrowed like Supergirl's would be, her jaw clenching and unclenching.

Will smirked, enjoying Stephanie's little show as he stood next to Jessica. Jessica took a step forward. "Back off, Drew," she said.

"Fine. I shouldn't have said 'bitch.' But this doesn't concern you," Drew said to Jessica. He turned his ire on Stephanie, staring her down. "Don't you have a Save the Whales fund-raiser to go to or something, Bergner?"

Stephanie didn't falter. She looked past Drew at Erin.

"Are you okay?" Stephanie asked.

"I'm fine," Erin spat. I couldn't tell if she was more upset with Stephanie than she was with Drew. "I'm driving home. You can get a ride from your *friends*, Drew, whom you wouldn't have if it weren't for me."

"Whatever, Erin." Drew ran his fingers over his buzz cut. "Just figure out if you want to spend any time with your boyfriend or not." He looked at Stephanie, who hadn't backed away. "What are you still looking at?"

He balled up his fists and leaned forward like he had when he was about to rush me.

"Hey, man, she's a girl. What are you doing?" I asked.

"A girl?" Stephanie yelled as she turned to face me. "I'm able to handle myself." Drew had at least eight inches and forty pounds on her. I stepped in front of Stephanie.

"Let's all calm down," I said as I walked Stephanie back to the bench. I didn't put my hands on her. I extended my arms to act as a barrier between her and Drew.

"Jeez, man," Drew said to me. "I don't know who you are for three years and now I have to see you every damn where. Why don't you go back to whatever country or Cave of Wonders you came from and leave me alone, okay?"

Whatever country I came from and an *Aladdin* reference. I didn't feel sorry for him anymore. I wanted to bust him in the mouth.

"Okay, Drew. I'll go back to where I came from," I said over my shoulder. "Back to your mom's house. She made me the best breakfast this morning after the time we had together last night. Her maple syrup tasted just as good as she did."

I turned around and Drew rushed me, knocking me to the sidewalk. I could hear Stephanie and Erin yelling for him to stop. I grabbed Drew by his fist and managed to press my forearm against his neck, holding him at bay. Will tugged Drew off me by the collar of his jacket. I jumped up. My hands trembled as adrenaline rushed through me.

"He's not worth it!" Will yelled at Drew, pushing him away from me. "You'll get him. Not like this, but you'll get him."

Drew and Will retreated to Will's car. I stood on guard until they got into the BMW.

"Are you hurt?" Stephanie asked. She rested her hand on my lower back. I shook my head, but she kept her hand there anyway. Jessica and Erin rushed over to me.

"I'm sorry," Erin said. She took a deep breath and ran her fingers through her hair.

"*I'm* sorry that you think it's in your best interest to spend time with that thug," Stephanie snapped at her.

"Don't yell at her! This is all your fault anyway," Jessica snapped back.

"You are both so frustrating," Erin said. She shook her head. It sounded like she was referring to more than the last five minutes.

"How is it my fault that her boyfriend is a jerk?" Stephanie asked.

"You provoke people," Jessica barked.

"I think if anyone was doing the provoking, it was Drew," I said.

"That's not what Will said about you two at practice," Jessica replied. "He said you started a fight with Drew and got him in trouble."

"I did not!" I said with a surprised laugh. Why would Will lie about that? "It wasn't even like that. He started it with me."

"That's probably why he was so agitated." She was blaming *me*?

"Hey, don't put this on me. It's not my fault your pals are threatened by my game."

Jessica's nostrils flared and her lips were pulled in tight.

"Can I give you a ride somewhere?" Erin asked me.

"I could use a ride, actually," I said, looking away from Jessica. "Like to a T stop, if that works?"

"I can take you to the one near Stephanie's place," Erin said.

"Erin, we were supposed to hang out tonight," Jessica said. "And how do you know where Bergner lives?"

"I don't need a ride, thank you," Stephanie said, her arms crossed in front of her. "I can call my father."

"It's part of the deal. I drop you off at home," Erin seemed to be reminding Stephanie. A deal? What kind of deal would these two have? Erin turned back to Jessica. "I'm sorry. I totally forgot about hanging out tonight," she said. She put her hands in her North Face's pockets. "I have a big test in two days, and I need more time to study."

Jessica gaped at her friend for a moment. "Okay. We'll hang some other time, when you don't have a test and you're not carpooling with people you barely know." She whipped around, her red ponytail almost hitting Erin in the face.

"Don't be mad, Jess," Erin called after her, but she didn't move to stop her. Stephanie still had her arms crossed over her chest. She kept her gaze fixed on the sidewalk and turned her head away when Erin tried to catch her attention.

"I'm not going to leave you here alone," Erin said.

It felt like if I didn't say something, they were going to stand outside the schoolhouse all night. "So . . . I could still use a ride. It's kind of chilly."

* * *

The silence in Erin's car was unbearable. I sat in the front seat but didn't dare touch the radio. I couldn't wait to tell Sean that I'd been a passenger in Erin Wheeler's super-nice ride. He wasn't going to believe me unless I could come up with a covert way to snag a selfie. Stephanie sat in the back, staring out the window as the suburbs turned into a city. Erin was driving out of her way for us.

"Nice wheels," I said to combat the uncomfortable silence.

"Thank you." Erin glanced up at her rearview mirror as if to check that Stephanie was still in the car. Stephanie was never so quiet.

"So your boyfriend is kind of a dick, huh?" I asked.

"So you kind of have it bad for Elle, huh?" Erin shot right back.

"Point taken, Reggie. Erin's personal life is none of Majidi's business."

"Is it that obvious?"

"Yes," both Erin and Stephanie responded.

"Oh! They read him like a Stephen King book at midnight on Halloween, Kevin!"

"Hey! She's back!" I turned to face Stephanie. "You guys want to grab some food? I'm starving."

"I doubt Erin would want to be seen in public with us," Stephanie said. She didn't bother to look at me; she just stared out her window. Erin didn't respond and the car became silent again.

"If you could drop me off here, that'd be great," I said as we approached the T stop at Coolidge Corner. Erin pulled over and put on her hazards. "Well, this was really weird."

"It sure was," Erin said. "But thanks for stepping in." Stephanie gave me a small wave from the backseat. I shut the door and hopped up to the platform to wait for the train. When I looked back at the car, Stephanie was getting out of the backseat and moving up front next to Erin. I didn't know a thing about girls.

* * *

I grabbed a carne asada burrito and a Coke after I got off the train at Davis Square. I scarfed the food-diaper down on the walk to my building and wiped my face as I rode the elevator up to the sixth floor.

I let myself in. Mom wasn't home yet. It was her book club night. I didn't know if they ever discussed books. From what I'd overheard the months when my mom hosted, book club seemed like an excuse for women to drink wine and talk about their lives or how great/lousy their kids/friends/partners/love lives were.

I dropped my backpack in my room and went to the bathroom, where I took off my shirt and checked myself out in the mirror. If I had any visible bruises from my fight with Drew, my mom would freak. There was a medium-sized purple bruise on the back of my right shoulder, but I could pass it off as a basketball injury.

I was at my desk doing my homework when Sean called.

"Man, you are never going to guess whose car I rode in today," I said right away.

He didn't bother guessing. "You haven't seen it yet, have you?"

"Seen what?"

"Check your Granger email."

I usually only checked my school email in the morning— for class assignments or announcements. Now I found a message with the subject "No Tradition of Violence." I guessed it had something to do with Stephanie's petition.

Why did Sean care? I didn't recognize the sender. I clicked the email open.

And there was my smiling face.

Decently photoshopped onto the head of a man with a long beard wearing a pakol hat and holding a gun.

The caption under the photo read, "Our New Mascot."

CHAPTER SIX

I had seen my mother really angry about three times in my life. The first time I don't remember so well. I was four. I must have blocked most of it out for self-preservation. She screamed at a doctor in the hospital when he told her that my dad had died of an aneurysm.

The second time was when I was eight and her parents visited. They asked her to move to LA and live with them. They didn't think she could handle work and taking care of me on her own. She had respectfully told them that we were fine, but they didn't listen until she swore in Farsi and banged her fists on the kitchen table. My grandma said she was behaving like a toddler. They made up the next day, but my grandparents didn't ask about our moving again.

The third time was in Headmaster Clarkson's office the morning after a photoshopped image of me as a terrorist was sent anonymously to the entire Granger student body. Only this anger was not loud like the other two times. This was a quiet rage, where every calm word dripped with fury.

"I want to know what you plan to do about all of this," Mom demanded. "What exactly are you doing to make sure whoever did this is punished?" She didn't want to give them any excuse to think of her as unreasonable or to say the minute she left the room, "You know how *those* people are." It's one of the many unspoken rules of complaining while not white.

I hadn't shown my mother the email. I didn't have to. By the time she got home from book club, Sean's mom Jane had called her. I wouldn't have said anything. When she asked me if I had any problems at school, I said no. It wouldn't be a good move as a new member of the varsity team to start accusing my teammates. I didn't tell her about my parking-lot skirmish with Drew either.

My mom and I weren't the only ones in Headmaster Clarkson's office that morning. Ms. Jacobs, the school guidance counselor, was there. Also in attendance: Ms. McCrea and the head of the board of trustees, Mr. Thompson. Yes, Will's grandfather and traditional mascot advocate Mr. Thompson. It probably goes without saying, but they're all white.

"As you know, Dr. Majidi, we at the Granger School have no tolerance for bullying of any kind," Headmaster Clarkson said. "That is a pact the families who send their children here make with the school upon admission, and we are investigating who is behind this with great urgency."

"I should hope so," my mom said, inching forward in her chair. "The whole point of sending my son here was for him to feel safe. That's why parents here pay tuition, isn't it? So our children can excel in a safe and nurturing environment? But you let this happen, Mr. Clarkson?"

"Unfortunately, we cannot control what students do off campus," Mr. Clarkson said.

"No, but you can certainly create a culture where students know this shouldn't happen," Mom argued. The room was silent until Mr. Clarkson spoke again.

"At this time, we have been unable to figure out who emailed the student body the, uh . . . the image," he continued. *The image.* Of me smiling like a goof while holding an AK-47. Great. Just great.

"Whoever sent the photo, according to our IT department, must be using a VPN," said Ms. Jacobs.

"What's that?" my mom asked, but in a gentler tone. Ms. Jacobs seemed to be sincerely upset by what had happened.

"*VPN* stands for Virtual Private Network. It's used to encrypt Internet traffic. Whoever sent that awful picture used a VPN router that hides their IP address. We can't tell where the email was sent from. The culprit's email address is not a Granger account and is linked to a Tor site that allows them to remain anonymous."

"You're saying there's no way of finding who did this?" My mom leaned forward.

"We aren't even sure it's a Granger student or anyone associated with Granger, are we, Jim?" Mr. Thompson asked, directing the question to Headmaster Clarkson. Mr. Thompson's willful ignorance was impressive.

"Who else, Mr. Thompson, would want to send that, and why would they send it to the Granger student body?" my mom asked. He opened his mouth to speak. I almost thought he was going to rattle off some conspiracy theory, but Ms. Jacobs bailed him out.

"Bijan," Ms. Jacobs began. I liked that she pronounced my name properly. The "Bi" like in *honeybee* and "jan" like in *January*. "Is there anyone who has been giving you a hard time lately?" It was the first time that morning anyone in the room had asked *me* anything.

Yes, somebody had been giving me a hard time, but it felt like regular team stuff. Once Drew got off me, I had thought more about my ride home in a luxury car and my delicious burrito than I had about what happened in the parking lot. But something had shifted when that image appeared on my screen. Since that moment, I had felt the weight of somebody else's living, throbbing, unimaginative hatred on my body. It sat like lead in my gut. Acid churned inside me, eating at my stomach. I felt sick, and I kept thinking:

Somebody *hates* me.

"No," I said, without making eye contact. I wasn't going to repeat what Will had said the day before—not with his all-powerful grandpa in the room now. I did want to know who sent the photo, though I had an idea it was Drew, but more than that, I wanted the whole thing to be over.

"We believe the email is linked to the campaign for changing the school's mascot that your son was participating in," Ms. McCrea said.

"Are you suggesting this is *his* fault?" my mom asked.

"No, no, not at all," Ms. McCrea said. I'd never understood how she was the dean of students when she really did not handle conflict well. "It is a theory that that may be why he was targeted."

"You think *that's* the only reason?" Mom turned her head to address Ms. McCrea. Ms. McCrea's face instantly went pink. "I understand this may be a new situation for you. But you invited my son here. He applied, he worked very hard, and you invited him to be a part of this institution. How do you plan to make him feel welcome?"

"Son, can you look at me a moment?" Mr. Clarkson said. Son? My father, in the few photographs we have of him, has warm eyes that look like he knew how to love me and see me. Headmaster Clarkson looked at me like he might be trying to remember a speech he had made long before to some other student whose name he had now forgotten.

"We are going to find whoever did this. I can promise you that," Mr. Clarkson said. "This nonsense, this bullying will not stand on our campus. We're going to do whatever we can to make sure nothing like this ever happens again, to you or to anyone else.

"I will be addressing the student body at the all-school assembly today," he continued, turning to Mom. "There will also be a formal letter sent to all the Granger families to convey our dismay at the situation and to remind them of our zero-tolerance policy when it comes to bullying—while keeping Bijan as anonymous as possible, of course."

This made my mom laugh. I stared at my lap.

"Headmaster Clarkson, how on earth could his anonymity stay intact when every student in the school has seen this photograph?" Mom asked.

At that moment, the bell rang, which meant all the students and faculty would be on their way to the auditorium for the morning assembly. This meeting was *finally* over.

"I will be following up," my mom said to Headmaster Clarkson. "I'm not letting this go."

The teachers stood only after my mom did. She and I exited the office together. Students were filing into the auditorium. Their collective chatter sounded louder to me today than it ever had before. Some of them noticed me and whispered to each other as they walked by. Didn't they realize that I could see them? That I knew they were talking about me?

My mom turned my cheek with her hand so that I would look down at her.

"You keep your head up today," she said in Farsi. I nodded. I understand Farsi but don't really speak it, even at home. My mom and I mostly communicate in English, but when she's upset or excited, or wants a little privacy, the Farsi comes through. "Remember what I've told you: if you let people walk over you once, expect to be trampled the next time. Okay?"

"I'll be okay," I muttered. I knew she was holding back on her impulse to hug me in front of everyone. She had been an American teenager once too.

"You text me if you need anything," she said in English. "We'll figure this all out when you get home." She turned around and walked down the hallway toward the exit. Students parted for her and then looked back at me. Yeah, that was my mom, and yeah, we'd been in the headmaster's office because of that photo. I stared at them until they kept walking.

Mr. Thompson was still talking to Headmaster Clarkson as they exited. They stopped when they saw me. Mr. Thompson gave me a quick nod like I was a problem for them to solve and be done with.

I joined the rest of the students shuffling into the auditorium and found my alphabetically assigned seat in the junior section. Sean was already in the seat next to mine. He'd kicked out my usual neighbor, James Lowell.

"Oh, hey! Weird bumping into you here," Sean said.

"Yep. Crazy coincidence."

"Anything happen last night?" Sean asked.

I played along. "Pretty uneventful."

"Do you want to ditch school today? I bet they'll let us." Sean flipped the bird to some sophomores gawking from their seats.

"Are you saying that as a supportive friend or because you're not ready for a test?"

"Can't it be both?" The auditorium was loud with conversations that I'm sure had everything to do with the email, but the people around me were quiet. Stephanie stood up in the front row and looked at me like I was some almost-extinct breed of tiger in a save-the-wildlife commercial. I could practically hear sad music playing in the background. I hated that. I didn't want to be pitied. I pretended I didn't see her.

"I got into it with Drew yesterday," I murmured to Sean.

"Did he come at you? I hope you got a punch in. He's first on my list."

"Huh?"

Sean pulled out a chart with caricatures he had drawn of every member of the varsity and JV basketball teams. He had also drawn Marcy, a cafeteria lady who usually looked at all of us like we were spoiled brats. Everyone had a thought bubble with a reason they might hate my guts. Some of the JV players were jealous that I'd made varsity before them. Kevin Donaldson, who was MIA from school because of his knee surgery, was on the chart with his leg in a cast. Drew's brow was furrowed in anger, and his cheeks were red. His thought bubble read, "I'm a douche. Reason enough."

"These are the suspects so far," Sean explained. "I didn't get to teachers, but they're next." The second bell rang. It was time to shut up and listen to morning announcements.

Headmaster Clarkson got onstage and stared down the student body until the auditorium grew disconcertingly silent. I suddenly felt like a suspect myself; Mr. Clarkson was looking at us like we were criminals. "I've been privileged to be an educator here for over two decades," he began in a booming voice. He never needed a microphone in this space. "In those twenty-plus years," he went on, "I've tried to express the values of our fair school to students and visitors. Values like integrity, community, honor, and service. I wonder if in all that time, in all the speeches, despite providing a space for students to achieve exemplary feats . . . I wonder if this year all of that has fallen on deaf ears."

"Looks like class is about to be in session, Kevin."

"Bring on the pain! Mad Dog Clarkson is ready to bite!"

"The email that was sent out last night was cruel and cheap, and could be considered criminal if reported to the authorities," Headmaster Clarkson continued. "It was an act of hate. Whoever participated in creating it wanted to touch everyone on this campus, and whoever created that piece of filth wanted to make sure that all of us felt it. Because hate doesn't just touch the intended target, it spreads to every person who witnesses it."

In front of me, I could see Stephanie nodding along as he spoke. The kid next to me, Charlie Martin, had the best seat in the house. He was so rigid, if I nudged him he'd shriek. He and I had history class together and exchanged pleasantries sometimes, but he couldn't even look at me this morning.

I got what Mr. Clarkson was saying, but it was kind of absurd at the same time. There was only one person in that photograph, and everyone in that auditorium knew it.

"We don't do this here!" Headmaster Clarkson shouted. "This is not who we are. This has never been who we are. This is not the Granger way." The guy sure had a lot of bulging veins in his neck. "I am not sure if we at Granger have taught you anything about respect for yourselves or for one another, but I can tell you this: whoever has decided they wanted to make this sick joke a part of the Granger legacy is going to be deeply disappointed and does not understand the severity of the punishment to come. I can assure you that the school will investigate this until the perpetrator or perpetrators are caught."

I looked over at the senior section. Will was chewing gum with his mouth open. Marcus was sitting forward in his seat with his hand covering his mouth. Todd was wide-eyed, bouncing his right leg up and down.

I could feel someone staring at me from behind. I turned a little, and sure enough, lots of students were paying attention to me instead of Mr. Clarkson. Noah averted his gaze when I stared at him.

Drew wasn't looking at me. He was staring at the back of the seat in front of him, not daring to look at the stage. His face was drained of color, except for the dark circles under his eyes.

He looked terrified.

CHAPTER SEVEN

After the assembly, I tried my best to join the crowds unnoticed, but that was impossible. The wide hallway was jammed with students. I could hear people talking about me everywhere, though they would stop speaking altogether when I walked by.

Sean stuck by my side like a five-foot-eight Secret Service agent. "Mom told me I'm driving you home after your practice today," he said as I tried to avoid eye contact with people.

"Huh? How come?"

"My moms are going to be at your place after work." Both of Sean's moms were friendly with my mom, but they weren't exactly close. "Come by the library after you're done at practice. Are you sure you don't want to ditch? I have Mom's car today; we could go to Newbury Comics."

It wasn't a bad idea. I didn't know how I was going to concentrate on much of anything with everyone looking at me like I was Dennis Rodman on my way to North Korea.

I stopped in front of my locker. "I think it's better to stick around. Let the jerk who sent that crap know I'm not going anywhere."

Elle Powell, girl of my dreams, came up to us, her backpack hoisted over one shoulder. "Hi, Bijan," she said.

"I am he. Yes. Hi."

"He is really struggling here. We have never seen him choke this badly in all of our commentating from his head!"

"I mean, hi. Hi, Elle." I closed my locker and leaned my arm on it to look casual. Sean sucked in his lips so as not to break out in hysterics.

A tiny smirk had formed on Elle's gorgeous face. Her hair was up in a bun and she wore pale purple lipstick. "How are you doing?"

"I'm not sure," I answered her honestly.

"That's the best he can come up with, Kevin? Come on, man!"

"This would probably be a good time to hear a word from our sponsors."

"My friend here is trying to say he's really happy to see you," Sean cut in. "Can I trust you with him while I get to class?"

"I'm headed in his direction," Elle said.

"Excellent! Please excuse his monosyllabic responses.

It only means he cares." With that, Sean slapped me on the back and left me to fend for myself.

"You sure you want to be around me today?" I asked her, doing my best to sound like a normal person as we walked side by side.

"I'm used to attention," she said kindly. "The way you played on Friday, I think crowds may be in your near future. Just be careful whom you decide to keep around you."

"You think I have what it takes to be a part of the in-crowd?" I said it like I was joking, but I really wanted to know what she thought of me.

"It's not all it's cracked up to be. Particularly if you don't exactly blend in the way they would like you to."

Some of the varsity ice hockey dudes walked by and scowled at me. I bit the inside of my cheek and held on to my backpack strap a little tighter. I could add them to Sean's chart.

"Anyway," Elle continued, "I wanted to tell you it was really messed up. The email." Right. She felt bad for me. Pity's not sexy. "I know we don't talk that often . . ."

"Oh my goodness, is he blushing? I think he's blushing!"

"She seems to be okay with it, Reggie!"

"What I'm trying to say is"—Elle leaned her shoulder in my direction—"if you want to talk about it, or not talk about it but have someone around to talk or not talk with you, that'd be okay with me."

70

I wanted to talk to her. I wanted to know everything about her and desperately wanted her to know everything about me. I wanted to know what her favorite song of all time was, and if she could travel anywhere in the world where would she want to go and could I go with her? I wanted her to know me better than anyone. I should have said that. Instead, all I got out was "Thanks."

We stopped outside our English classroom. The students filing in looked at us as they walked by. They were probably still thinking of the email. Yeah, take a long look, creeps.

"I think I should have ditched school for the comics shop with Sean today," I said.

"But it's not even new comic Wednesday," Elle said. "You can close your mouth. Yes, women read comics. We even make them. Jeez."

I didn't realize my jaw had dropped.

"No, I know that. I didn't think *you* read comics, though. I mean, your reading selections are always so *literary*," I said.

"Comics and graphic novels can be literary too. But now it's time to discuss *The Scarlet Letter*," Elle said, tilting her head to our class.

"That Dimmesdale has a lot of nerve," I replied.

"Oh?"

"Yeah! I mean, he knows what he did. *He knows*." I widened my eyes for comical effect. "Besides, I only pay attention when you read your stuff, anyway."

"That was smooth!"

"They even exchanged multiple sentences, Reggie."

"Is she blushing this time, Kevin?"

"Oh my goodness, she is!"

"Cute. That's cute," she said with a shy grin before she walked into class.

"Do you believe in miracles?"

"Wrong sport, Kevin."

* * *

The bell rang, signaling the end of a long day of classes. I still had practice, but I was keener to run around and deal with stress that way than I'd been to have well-meaning teachers not know what to say in my presence. Most of my teachers had continued with their lesson plans, not addressing the day's weirdness.

Ms. McCrea spent the *whole* class period trying to get us to open up about whether we felt the school was a safe and welcoming community. I felt like shouting, "Obviously not, Ms. McCrea!" but I didn't want to be the suffering kid there to teach the other students a life lesson. I wanted to know what was going to be on the quiz the next day.

I tried to ignore people whispering. My favorite bit of overheard gossip came from a freshman kid outside the science lab: "I heard he's, like, a prince from Dubai or something." Man, if I were a prince from Dubai, the *hell* would I be doing here?

"Bijan!" Stephanie shouted from the other end of the hall. She waved her arm and began to rush toward my locker. I took my sports bag out and slammed the little metal door as fast as possible but couldn't escape. "I'm so glad I found you. I was hoping to speak with you about your ordeal. Now, I was thinking the best course of action would be to have some sort of rally to mobilize the student body and show that Islamophobia and xenophobia are unacceptable—"

"Whoa, hold up," I said, raising both my hands. "The last time I helped you 'mobilize the student body,' I got my face plastered on everyone's computer screens." She looked at me like I was speaking Farsi. "Also, I'm doing okay, all things considered. Thanks for asking."

Stephanie's face fell. She blushed and put her hand over her heart. "I'm sorry. I don't really . . . I sometimes say too much. Or want to say too much. I didn't mean to be insensitive." She looked dejected, her shoulders slumped and her cheeks red. She made it hard to be mad at her sometimes. *Sometimes.*

"I want to forget the whole thing. Thank you for your interest in bringing awareness or whatever, but I . . . I don't want to be one of your projects."

Stephanie winced.

"Ooooh, that is quite the accusation, Kevin. Looks like the rookie has some trust issues."

"Do you . . . do you really think that's why I'm concerned

about what's happened to you? Because I think of you as a project?"

I looked at my shoes and shrugged.

"Hi, guys," Noah said, appearing from out of nowhere, like he had a GPS tracker in Stephanie's backpack. He wore a smile like a game show host's, sincere enough to let you believe he wanted you to win the Jet Skis, but casual enough that you knew it wouldn't be any skin off his nose when you didn't. "How you doing, Beej?"

"You know, still alive, so can't complain," I said.

Noah didn't even acknowledge I'd said anything but zeroed in on Stephanie. "I can bring my car out front so you don't have to walk to the lot in the cold."

"Oh, thank you, Noah, but I won't be needing a ride home today."

"Why not? You don't have any clubs or lessons this afternoon." Wow. He had her schedule memorized?

"I'm going to be in the library," she replied. Stephanie's tone was cordial, but she took one step back from him.

"I can wait until you're finished. I have homework to do too." This exchange was as painful as watching the Celtics lose in blowouts to the Cavs during playoffs.

"I am helping someone with their studies." This time, she was curt.

There was a split second when it looked like Noah was unaware of where he was or how to form words. He looked so . . . vacant. When he smiled at her again, it was taut and forced. "No worries! I'll see you tomorrow, then," he said before he strode past us to the front entrance.

"Is he always so, um, persistent?" I asked.

Stephanie cleared her throat and looked a little flushed. "He has a tendency to be overprotective. He's keenly aware of what people say about me."

"Because he has a thing for you."

"I don't think that's true," she said. She picked a piece of lint off her shirt so she wouldn't have to look at me.

"What town does he live in?" I asked as we turned and headed down the hall.

"Dover," she replied.

"And you live in Brookline, right?" Both were affluent suburbs, only Dover was farmlike and quiet, and Brookline, which was technically part of the city, was a bustling metropolis.

"Obviously, you know that from our little carpool trip yesterday," Stephanie said. We made our way outside to the quad. The end of February meant spring might not be around for another two months, and that was if we New Englanders were lucky. I zipped my jacket up all the way to my chin.

"He drives you home how often?"

"It depends . . ." she said reluctantly. "Mostly once a week." She pulled her peacoat tighter around her.

"You're telling me dude drives against traffic to bring you home? That's, like, an hour and a half of his day devoted to driving you around. You don't think he's maybe got a thing for you?"

"There isn't any romance there!" she said, waving her hands in front of her like she did when she was making a speech in assembly. "He's usually working with me on community projects, so it makes sense to carpool sometimes. Noah and I are friends."

"Then what are you and Erin?" I asked. "She drives you home too, but she doesn't even like talking to you in public." It came out nastier than I wanted it to.

She didn't have an answer for me. I had figured out a way to shut Stephanie Bergner up.

"I've got to get to practice," I said, hoping she wouldn't follow me all the way to the gym.

* * *

When I opened the door to the locker room, I mentally braced myself for some dirty looks and insults from Will and Drew. I slipped into the room and quietly closed the door behind me, making my way toward the lockers. I missed the old days on JV, where there was some lighthearted trash talk, jokes about someone's overuse of Axe body spray, and theories on what would happen if you smeared Icy Hot all over your junk.

The conversation around the varsity lockers was subdued. Guys were talking one at a time, not over each other.

"I don't know, maybe that email was a warning or something," I heard Will say. "Like someone was trying to tell us something about him."

I stopped walking. I looked around and found some freshman from the JV squad staring at me wide-eyed.

"What do you mean, a warning?" Todd asked.

"Like he's up to something and someone is trying to tell us before it's too late," Will said. "You never know, man. I mean, people get radicalized, right? Maybe somebody knows something about that dude that we don't. You should have seen him yesterday when he got into it with Drew."

"I think you've been drinking a little too much fear and propaganda punch, Will," Marcus said.

"Come on, Marcus. What do we really know about him? I mean, he keeps to himself. He never partied with us. When he does talk, he always says some goofy stuff that doesn't make any sense," Will continued.

What did he want me to do? Show up to parties I was never invited to? Did he want me to, I don't know . . . be jollier during that one practice I had attended? Especially when grunting and sweating during drills? Maybe he'd prefer I go through a metal detector while saying the pledge of allegiance before entering the gym?

"He's our teammate now," Marcus said. "That's what I know about him."

I couldn't stand there forever, but I didn't know how to interrupt a conversation about whether I was a threat to national security. I could have coughed. Or whistled, to let them know I was a carefree kind of guy. I didn't do either of those things. Instead, I walked over, pretending I hadn't heard anything.

"'Sup?" I said, doing that raising-of-the-chin thing varsity guys always do. I don't know if it looks good when I do it. I feel like it's so forced.

"Hey," Marcus said. He was the only one to greet me.

I could feel eyes on me when I emptied the contents of my bag into my locker. Maybe they were looking for a weapon of mass destruction, but all I had was a T-shirt, Right Guard deodorant, and a pair of shorts. Drew wasn't in the locker room. He probably didn't want to face me after sending that email. The chump. I'd take care of him on the court. At least there was one less "teammate" in the locker room to deal with.

"Hey, B. So, like, what are you?" Will asked. He took long strides to stand behind me, leaning against the lockers while I loosened my tie.

I knew what he was getting at. He hadn't asked it as eloquently as others had, but I'd gotten versions of this question plenty of times before, and this wouldn't be the last. I could make it a little hard for him, though.

"I'm a human being," I said as I unbuttoned my dress shirt. "Last I checked." Marcus and a few others chuckled at that.

"But I mean, you know, where are your people from?"

He was closing in on me. Maybe I should have told him what he wanted to hear. My mom was from Southern California, but her parents were from Iran. My dad was from Jordan. His family, whom I didn't see very often after his passing, lived in Jordan, Germany, and Canada.

"Somerville," I replied. I could feel his breath on my neck. "I appreciate your sudden interest in me, but I'm about to take off my pants, so maybe I could have a little space?"

"Majidi is playing with fire here, Reggie."

"Well, what do you expect, Kevin? You think he's going to keep taking what they're dishing out and ask for more with a smile?"

Will backed up. "You know what I mean, dingus," he said.

"I sure do," I said with as much acid as possible. I turned around and stared at him. "Where's your buddy? He planning on jumping me again today, or is that just on days when he's picking on girls?"

"Drew's in Coach's office because of you. Probably getting his ass handed to him for no reason."

"If he sent out that crap about me, then that's the reason," I said.

"Maybe he did, maybe he didn't. Whoever did send it, I'd love to shake their hand and buy them a beer," Will said with a snarl.

"I'd love to buy a keg for whatever college will take you," I spat back. "How much does your grandpa pay to

79

have you play for us? Can't he buy off some place of higher education? I'll chip in, get a collection going."

Will lunged at me, but Steve pulled him back, and after a second, he remembered where he was. Will wasn't as naive as Drew. He wouldn't try anything on school grounds. Fighting on campus could lead to expulsion. I didn't snitch, but I was sure Drew and Will knew I could.

"Will, that's enough!" Marcus interrupted. "Lead the guys out to the court."

Will stared at me for an uncomfortable few seconds before he and our lingering teammates went out.

Marcus stayed behind. "Fun day for you, I bet."

"The funnest," I replied.

"Don't let people get to you so much that you forget about grammar." Marcus adjusted the ACE bandage on his knee. "Is this your first brush with the ever-rampant cancer known as racism?"

"No. But it's never been this specifically viral before." I pulled on my practice jersey.

"Has your mom given you the 'don't wear hoodies or play loud music when you go out' speech? Or is that just for us black sons?"

"I got the 'shave before you go to the airport and don't read anything in Farsi or Arabic when you're out of the house' speech. Not that I can read either language anyway." I slammed my locker door and banged my fist on the metal.

"Go easy on that hand. We're going to need you to win that New England championship, and the next two games. Excellence shuts everybody up real quick. I'll see you out there."

Marcus left me alone to finish getting ready.

CHAPTER EIGHT

Practice was brutal. Coach had us run suicides for twenty minutes, his way of punishing us for being part of something stupid. He didn't give us a speech about team unity or anything. From the look on Drew's ashen face and the way he carefully avoided making eye contact with me, I guessed Coach had already made his speeches for the day. But when practice ended, Coach asked me to come to his office instead of showering with the rest of the team. If he didn't mind my BO, that was fine by me. I didn't want to face everyone in the locker room again anyway, but I was all too aware that I'd gone two for two in post-practice office chats. If this was going to be a regular thing, I'd have to let my ride know. I had already missed the bus once; I didn't want to make Sean wait too.

I sat across from Coach. There were two old photos on his desk. One was of a much younger and thinner Coach with a player in a Sacramento Kings uniform. Coach must have worked with him. The other photo was of a maybe ten-year-old girl hugging the same version of Coach.

"Is that your daughter?" I asked.

"Yes." He didn't offer any information about her. "How you doing, kid?"

"I've been better," I answered, because "kind of crappy" wouldn't have been appropriate.

"I bet. It's a shame what kids can do these days with computers. I thought we gave you all too much home-work. I mean, what jerk would find the time, you know?" It wasn't exactly a condemnation. "Did you and Drew have words after you left here yesterday?"

I took a beat. I couldn't decide if I should tell Coach what had happened.

"What did he say?"

"He said you two were fine, you didn't see each other after you left my office." Either Coach was lying or Drew had lied to him earlier. "I don't think he sent that email."

"What makes you say that?"

"He knows enough not to do anything to jeopardize his being a student here. You got here because of your brains. Drew is here because I made it happen."

"We get it, Coach. You're the head honcho."

"You've got to wonder about a coach who speaks so disparagingly about his player, Reggie. Not exactly the kind of guy you want to mentor kids."

"He also works at some pizza restaurant most nights after practice. He said he was working last night. But again, I don't really know what transpired between you two after you left here."

I didn't think Coach actually *wanted* to know if Drew and I fought after practice the day before. If he knew, Drew might get suspended, and if he got suspended, he couldn't play. "Now, you have to trust that the faculty are going to find out who did this, and you have to be patient."

"And wait until after playoffs, right, Coach?"

"It seems that's what he's saying, Reggie."

"I want to play, Coach. That's it. I don't want beef with anybody." What I wanted to say was "I can't help it if somebody has a problem with my existence. I can't solve that for you."

"Good. That's good. We're going to need you focused for this week's game."

* * *

I took the world's fastest shower before meeting Sean in the library. I had pulled on a Celtics knit hat so I wouldn't have icicles for hair, but I didn't have anything to block the frosty air hitting my face. I entered the warm library, grateful for some reprieve from the unrelenting winter. The musty smell of old books struck me with a wave of nostalgia for the reading room at the Somerville public library. When I was a kid, my mom used to take me there all the time. I think I made her read me the Frog and Toad books a million and one times, but she never got tired of the same stories. Maybe she did, but I couldn't tell when she did the voices.

I waved at the librarian, Ms. Spooner, who sat behind the front desk of an otherwise pretty dead building. She whispered hello to me, even though there was nobody in there to disturb. The couches up front by the magazines and newspaper racks are usually occupied during study periods but were empty this late.

I took off my hat and searched for Sean between the rows of bookshelves toward the back. A peal of laughter came from one of the study rooms. The door to the study room was halfway open, and I peeked in. Erin Wheeler sat at a table, laughing uncontrollably. I'd never seen her so at ease and uninhibited before. Even Will sometimes gave Drew a hard time about it at practice, asking why Drew could never manage to make his girlfriend smile.

"Hey! Over here," Sean said, from a table farther down. He didn't even bother to whisper. It got Erin's attention. When she looked up and saw me, she stopped laughing. Her face looked like I had walked in on her on the toilet.

The person who must have made Erin laugh poked her head out the door. "Could you please keep it dow—" Stephanie broke off when she saw me.

Sean walked over to me with his backpack in hand and looked into the study room. "Unusual study buddies," he said, intrigued.

Erin composed herself. Her smile vanished and her expression settled into its usual resting bitch face. Stephanie crossed her arms over her chest and looked a little annoyed.

"Hi. Sorry. We didn't mean to, uh, interrupt," I said as Stephanie stood up.

"That's quite all right. We were taking a much-needed break from our tutoring session." I've never gotten that much joy from studying, but I didn't say anything.

"Hey," Erin offered weakly. If Stephanie had been tutoring Erin, it made sense that Erin had gotten her grades up. Erin took her phone from her pocket and checked it like we didn't exist.

"How'd practice go?" Sean asked me.

"I didn't get in a fistfight today. Just some trash talk." Stephanie watched our conversation closely. She opened her mouth briefly before she decided she wanted to listen instead of speak for once. I turned to her and Erin. "We were about to head out."

"Did Drew give you a hard time?" Erin asked without looking away from her phone.

"Your boyfriend was well behaved."

"Good." Erin looked up from her phone and made eye contact with Stephanie. I wanted to ask her if Drew really did have work after practice, but the last thing I needed was Stephanie launching an investigation on my behalf, most likely making the situation even worse. "He's also not my boyfriend anymore."

Stephanie's eyes widened, and so did mine. I guess it was news to both of us. I thought it was kind of cool. Drew had acted like an ass and had probably sent the photo of me. He deserved to be dumped. Stephanie just stood there, shocked.

"I guess you have a ride home, then," I said to Stephanie. She blushed and didn't answer me as Sean and I made our exit.

* * *

Sean had WERS, the college radio station, on in his mom's Prius as we left the burbs for the city. Funk music filled the silence in the car.

"What was with you and Stephanie at the library?" Sean asked as he merged onto the highway.

"Nothing," I said. I was pissed off, but I shouldn't have taken it out on her like that.

"I wouldn't mind tutoring Erin Wheeler," Sean said, tapping his fingers on the steering wheel to the music. "I'd answer any anatomy and physiology questions she may have."

I didn't have the energy to fake a chuckle, but he didn't seem to mind.

"Do you ever feel like you don't really know anybody?" I asked. "Like you see people every day, but you don't know anything about them?"

"I think we get to know whom we want to know." It didn't seem to bother Sean that we went to school with racists. "Most people aren't worth knowing. It's the Age of the Asshole, man. It's their time to shine. Doesn't matter what race, religion, orientation, or gender. If you're a jerk, the world is yours for the taking."

I didn't bother to argue with him. Maybe a few days before, I would have. "Why don't we become jerks too?"

"We could. Maybe we already are," Sean said, waggling his eyebrows. I felt a twist of guilt in my stomach. "But let me ask you this: Do you feel good when you pull a jerk move?"

I thought about Stephanie's face when I left the library. I had made her feel just as bad as Drew or Erin did. "No."

"Well, maybe we live another day to be decent human beings. Besides, jerks always look like they're constipated. You can tell from their faces. They're always pinched."

"Please don't major in philosophy when you go to college."

"I don't need to major in it. Teach it, maybe, but you don't need class to study life. Besides, I was thinking of art school."

"Your moms are going to hate that," I said.

"Don't I know it," Sean said as we sat stalled in traffic.

* * *

We opened my front door to find a bunch of parents, some of whom I didn't even recognize, on their phones, stuffing envelopes, and talking. My living room was like a campaign office in late October. This really wasn't what I wanted to come home to. All I wanted was heated-up leftovers and Sports Center with my mom after I finished my homework.

"Hi, boys." Sean's Mama Hana came to the door and gave us both a hug. "There's pizza in the kitchen."

"What's going on?" I asked.

"What kind of pizza?" Sean asked.

Both his mother and I stared at him. I knew that whatever this was, it had to do with the stupid email, but I wasn't sure how it had led to an eighty-person letter writing campaign. Okay, there were maybe ten people, but it felt like more.

"You know what, I'll go and grab us some food." Sean slapped my back before escaping into the kitchen.

"How are you doing, Bijan?" Sean's mom asked, taking my hand and staring up at me. I knew she cared, but it had been less than a day and I was already sick of people looking at me with doleful eyes.

"I'm okay."

"Why don't you come over and talk to your mom and Jane." Mama Hana led me through the living room. I tried to match parents with their kids at Granger. There was a woman on the phone whom I recognized from some of the basketball games from when I was a fan and not a player. She looked exactly like Marcus when he focused on his free-throw shots. There was a short man who was speaking superfast to a few women and blinking a lot. I figured he must be related to Stephanie. Genes are weird.

It was like a party. My mom set two fruit and cheese plates on our coffee table for guests who were on the couch folding letters and licking envelopes. When she stood back up, she finally noticed me. She gave me a big hug, which was a little embarrassing.

As Mom let go of me, Sean's other mother, Jane, stood up from the couch.

"Hey, kiddo," she said. "How you doing?" I should have had a T-shirt that read I FEEL LIKE CRAP.

"Fine," I said.

"Hana and Jane were kind enough to help me organize this evening," Mom said, oblivious to how uncomfortable the whole thing was making me.

"What exactly is 'this evening'?"

"Why don't we find somewhere private to talk," Jane suggested. I looked around. Where we were supposed to find somewhere private?

My mom led us to the kitchen, where Sean was sitting at our table, stuffing his face with pizza directly from the box.

"Sean, use a plate, please," Jane said. Sean finished his slice, ignoring his mom's request. I sat down next to him. I usually live for pizza, but even the smell was making me nauseous. I couldn't stomach the thought of eating with my insides in knots.

"We're following up our emails with formal letters to organize the Granger parents. The letters inform parents that we've requested a meeting with the board to discuss ways to make the school a safer space." My mom sounded like she had rehearsed that all day. "Jane and Hana were able to bring some volunteers to help spread the word."

"We're with you one hundred percent, Bijan," Jane said. "There are a lot of us who want to nip this thing in the bud."

"We also want to explain some legal aspects to you and your mother," Hana added.

"Hang on a sec—legal aspects?" I asked, looking at my mom.

Mom took a deep breath. She looked more exhausted than usual. That morning she'd been alert, ready to kick butt. Now she looked worn down. I felt guilty to be somehow responsible for that. Isn't that messed up? Someone harms my mom and me and I felt guilty about it. "Hana explained to me that because there wasn't an explicit threat of violence against you, what was sent can't technically be categorized as a hate crime, but it is a bias-motivated incident. We can notify the Massachusetts attorney general's office or file a civil rights complaint."

They were making all these plans without even asking if it was okay with me. Without asking if I wanted my living room full of people I didn't know treating me like a charity case.

"Mom, may I speak to you for a minute? Alone?" I asked.

* * *

"Your room is such a mess," my mom said, looking at the clothes, both clean and dirty, strewn across my floor.

"Even in times of crisis, Reggie, Mama Bear takes the time to comment on her son's hygiene."

"Which reminds me: when you've gone nose blind, use Febreze!"

"Mom, don't you think this has kind of gotten out of hand?" I flopped down on my bed. "I want the whole thing to blow over. People will forget about it soon."

"I see," she said, quirking one eyebrow and putting her hands on her hips like she was Wonder Woman. I knew she didn't actually "see" at all. "There are a lot of parents who send their children to your school who find it very difficult to let a hateful act like this . . . how did you put it? 'Blow over'?"

She was expecting me to give in, to say "Fine," like I did in most of our arguments. But this wasn't fine. "Those parents don't have to attend high school every day with kids whose parents *won't* be at that meeting."

My mom interlocked her fingers in front of her mouth. This was her "I'm about to put you in your place" pose. I had readied myself for her lectures before. Sometimes I stare at her chin and pretend I'm listening when I'm really making myself think about how I hate the sound of cold cuts being pulled apart from each other or slapped together or other random stuff like that. This time, though, I paid attention. I had to argue with her if I was ever going to get her to stop.

"So let me ask you," she started. "If this were happening to another student at Granger, would you ignore it?"

It didn't happen to another student at Granger, Mom. It happened to me. I didn't say that out loud, but I shouldn't have had to.

"If this happened to one of your friends, if it happened to Sean, would you sit idly by? Would you be comfortable with your own complacency while your friend was being dehumanized?" She was good. Maybe she should have studied law instead of dentistry. "I received so many calls, so many emails from parents today. A lot of people I didn't know, parents of children in different grades, from all different backgrounds. They told me about the discussions they're going to be having in their homes tonight. This is bigger than you, Bijan. I know it hurts you. I know you want to forget about it. But this is bigger than you."

I couldn't look at her. I knew she was right. But it also hurt that she wouldn't let me process this in my own time. It hurt a lot.

"Whatever. Just don't include me in your meetings, okay?" Being at assembly with everyone either looking at me or doing their best to pretend I wasn't there was all I could stomach. I didn't want to be a symbol for the Justice League of Parents to use in their crusade to eradicate campus intolerance.

She sat down on the bed next to me. "Maybe it's my fault," she said, shrugging. "Maybe I didn't give you enough pride in where your family comes from. Both of your parents are from cradles of civilization. Thousands of years of culture on both your father's side and mine. You're the son of rich histories. You are from the places where numbers and language were born."

"Nobody at Granger cares about that, Mom," I said. "I don't want to be the poster child for this!" To the kids at Granger, I looked like an extra for Claire Danes to chase down in some alley for information. To them, I looked like a kid Bradley Cooper would have in the crosshairs of his gun. To them, I looked like I didn't belong at their school. They didn't know the difference between any of the Middle Eastern, South Asian, or North African countries. They didn't know anything about the different cultures, languages, or histories, and honestly, it felt like they didn't want to know.

"If your father were here—"

"Don't!" I shouted. "Don't pull the dad card on me." We were both surprised. My mom usually didn't bring my dad up unless I asked her to. When I was a kid, I asked about him a lot, but the older I got, the less point there seemed to be. All I knew of my father was stories. The more time passed, the less sure I was whether he was someone I would have loved or someone I would have rebelled against. Or both.

Youssef Haddad, my father, whom I barely knew, but whom I thought about more often than I admitted to my mom. We hadn't even kept his last name after he passed. It's still on my birth certificate, but at school, my mom thought it'd be easier to go by her last name. That, or she didn't want to be painfully reminded that he wasn't here every time someone said my full name. I get that there isn't always an easy fix for grief. People have different ways of coping. But I don't think my mom and I have figured out how to cope together.

We have a few videos of him, which I make sure to watch when Mom isn't around. One is of their wedding. The ceremony was Persian. My parents sat at a *sofreh aghd*. Women my mom used to be friends with held a linen cloth above them and ground sugar over it so my parents would have a sweet life together. Mom doesn't hang out with those women anymore. I guess when Dad died, that part of her life died too.

For their reception, they had a *zaffa*, an Arabic wedding procession. Three drummers led them into a hotel ballroom, announcing their arrival as a married couple to a room full of people I'm related to but have never met. It looks like a hell of a party. The guests stand up and cheer before joining the dancing. You can see my dad proudly mouthing "Look at my wife!" several times throughout the night. I've memorized everything he says in those videos.

He looks like he's having the time of his life.

My mom looks light. She doesn't have the weight of the universe on her shoulders yet.

Now, standing in my room arguing with me, she looked stuck. Stuck with me.

"Sorry," I said. "There's . . . He's not here. There's no point in bringing him up." I didn't say it to hurt her, but the way she flinched told me that I had. I waited for her to argue with me.

"You don't have to do anything you don't want to do," she said quietly. "But the meeting is happening. I would like for you to be there." Then she left me alone in my room to stare at my posters of Steph Curry and Kyrie Irving. I wondered if their moms knew how to guilt trip them like a boss too.

CHAPTER NINE

After a week of classes, practice, Mom's endless phone calls to other parents, and paranoia occupying my every stray thought, Friday arrived. Game day.

On big game days, we were allowed to wear Granger sports gear instead of our usual school uniform of khaki pants, white shirts, ties, and boat shoes. Only, today was different. I looked around the auditorium during assembly to find about forty or so students wearing the HERE TO STAY shirts, the Gunner logo proudly displayed on their torsos. About twice as many wore the NO TRADITION OF VIOLENCE shirts. I hadn't gotten the memo. I was wearing my track pants and a Granger sweatshirt that had the school's name on it and nothing else.

When assembly was over, the staff of the *Granger Gazette* passed out the new issue of the paper to the student body.

Everyone walked slowly, reading as they made their way to their first period.

"Whoa, Beej, you're on the front page," Sean said, handing me a paper. Below the fold was a great snapshot of me being held up by my teammates after our win against Carter Prep. The caption read, "Granger Boys' Basketball Triumphant After Dramatic Last-Minute Basket by Newcomer Bijan Majidi." For a moment I was proud. I was good enough at basketball to make the front page!

Then I saw the headline above the fold for another article and my stomach sank.

"Mascot Controversy Sparks Hate Incident."

I skimmed the article. It explained that an email had been sent anonymously, depicting a student in the mascot's image. It didn't show a photo of the email or mention me by name, but I thought it was kind of lousy that they put a photo of me from the game right below the article that was meant to keep me anonymous. Thanks for respecting my privacy, *Granger Gazette*!

The article about the email did have some choice quotes from anonymous sources, like "I'm sorry about what happened to that kid, but people feel strongly about this stuff. You can't mess with tradition" and "I don't get what everyone is complaining about. It's not like the mascot is literally shooting anyone." There was only one student who went on the record.

"I think it is shameful but very telling of the climate at Granger that someone felt entitled to do something as egregious as send that email," said Stephanie Bergner, creator of the No Tradition of Violence campaign. "I am hurt by that image, as every student at Granger should be." When Bergner was asked if the campaign would continue, she responded, "I plan to continue. I never intended for anyone to get hurt by this endeavor."

I handed the paper back to Sean. I wasn't going to read more of what Stephanie or anyone else had to say about that stupid mascot. Sean continued to read as he leaned on the locker next to mine.

"The *Gazette* doesn't have any leads on who did it," Sean said. No kidding. It's a high school paper, not the *Boston Globe*. It's not like they have real investigative journalists at their disposal. No one from the paper had come to talk to me or let me know they'd be running the article.

I walked down the hall and noticed notes and plastic bags of candy taped to some of the lockers. On game days, members of the girls' varsity team would leave treats for the boys' varsity team and vice versa. When I opened my locker, I was hoping I'd find a note of encouragement or some treats from a secret psych. But there was nothing new in my locker. Just my math textbook, a photo of Sean and me dressed up as Ghostbusters for Halloween, and an extra set of clothes I hadn't put in my sports bag yet. I guess I shouldn't have expected anything, but it would have been kind of cool.

* * *

My last class of the day was US History. We took our quizzes in silence while Ms. McCrea paced the classroom. It had been a weird week. I hadn't studied very much for anything, and I wasn't doing so hot on the quiz.

"Okay, that should be enough time. Pass in your papers, please." Ms. McCrea finally took a seat at her desk. Our desks were arranged in a U shape because Ms. McCrea said that being able to see each other facilitated discussion. We shuffled our papers hand to hand around the U until they made it to Ms. McCrea.

"How'd you do?" I asked Sean, who sat next to me.

"Nailed it. Either that or I failed horribly. Could go either way, based on subjectivity and revisionist history," Sean murmured.

Ms. McCrea took all the quizzes and held them to her chest like they were her teddy bear. "I will cherish these for the rest of my life. Or return them to you tomorrow," she said before putting them in her tote bag.

"So today we're going to resume our discussion on Executive Order 9066, which, after the bombing of Pearl Harbor, resulted in the internment of American citizens and permanent residents, many of whom were children. These citizens and residents had to leave their homes and their businesses and were imprisoned in camps. In most cases, people lost their property, their businesses, their college careers. Their lives were forever changed. People were forced to live in oftentimes unsanitary conditions and their humanity was stripped away. The detention centers were overcrowded, surrounded by barbed wire, guarded by military personnel—"

Jessica Carter raised her hand. "You forgot to mention they were Japanese," she blurted out, not waiting to be called on.

"Should that matter?" Ms. McCrea asked the class.

"Well, we were at war with Japan, so . . ." Charlie Martin, my assembly companion, answered.

"But the people put in camps were American," Ms. McCrea responded. "They were of Japanese ancestry, but they had built lives in America. They were part of American communities."

"In the textbook, it explains that the government was worried that there might have been spies within the Japanese communities," Jessica said. She had blue and gold ribbons hanging from her pigtails but was in her school uniform. I was surprised she wasn't wearing a HERE TO STAY shirt.

"So paranoia justifies rounding up thousands of people and treating them like prisoners?" Ms. McCrea asked, staring at her.

"It was wartime, we'd been attacked, our government did what it needed to do," Jessica said. "I'm not saying it was a perfect idea. I get that innocent people suffered, but maybe it did help in some way. Who knows?"

"I'll remember you said that next time I see you post a photo at Benihana," Sean spat back. A few people chuckled nervously.

Jessica turned and looked not at Sean but directly at me. "War is not politically correct or polite. It's a time when you have to do what's necessary to protect people."

"How long does a person or group of people have to live in the U.S. before they are considered truly American, Jessica?" Sean asked. "I have a feeling you would have *loved* the House Un-American Activities Committee. Such a shame you weren't around to be a member."

Jessica didn't answer. She kept staring at me.

My skin didn't just crawl; it felt like it was going to leap off my body, turn to liquid, and seep into the floorboards.

"The only group of people who are truly original Americans are Native Americans," Charlie said. He likes to hike up his participation grade by playing both sides of an issue.

"Yes, and look how well they've been treated." Sean's voice dripped with sarcasm.

"It's true, America is a country with a history of injustice, but can we learn from those injustices? Make sure our society is indeed democratic and fair to all who reside here?" Ms. McCrea asked the room. "The internment camps are a horrendous blight on our founding principles. Let's remember that while these things have happened in the past, and it may be difficult to imagine, these were real people with real lives."

"Typical. Any time we have a discussion, it has to fit a certain agenda," Jessica said, rolling her eyes.

"An agenda?" Ms. McCrea asked. "Jessica, while we are free to speak, we must do so with respect," she said.

Jessica still huffed.

"I think I get what Jessica is saying. No one feels like they can say anything out of fear of saying the wrong thing," Charlie put in.

"Sometimes it *is* the wrong thing," Sean responded.

"When there are threats to national security, foreign or domestic, the government has to do what it feels necessary to make sure Americans are safe," Jessica said. "Whether it offends people or not, hard decisions have to be made."

"So people's civil liberties can go to hell so long as we're safe, yeah?" Sean asked. "Fascism is a slippery slope, isn't it, Ms. McCrea?"

"So it is," Ms. McCrea said, her face drained of color. I guess she hadn't expected class comments to throw a wrench into her lesson plan.

The bell rang. Jessica smirked at us before she stood up and left.

"Hey, guys, wait up a minute," Ms. McCrea said to Sean and me as we stood up. "I know things got a little testy today. I think I need to reframe my questions next time. But dialogue is always good. There's no solution without communication."

"Depends on what's being communicated," Sean said. He and I walked out of the classroom. I thought for sure Ms. McCrea would ask Sean to stay to discuss things further, but she just let us go.

Jessica and Will stood by his locker, hugging. When she saw us heading down the hallway, she leaned over and whispered something in Will's ear. He looked up and glared at me from across the hall. What a great couple they made.

"I told you, man," Sean said. "It's the Age of the Asshole."

"You said it," I agreed.

I didn't want to be a part of it, though. I had to go talk to Stephanie, try to make things right between us. I shouldn't have insulted her when she was trying to reach out, even if I didn't want to be part of her "endeavor." I saw Noah farther down the hallway, exiting a class. "Hey, Noah!"

He looked surprised but immediately put on his game-show-host smile.

"Hey, Beej," he said. "How's it going?"

"Not bad, thanks. You?" I wanted to get the pleasantries out of the way.

"Been busy with the *Gazette* since the mascot campaign picked up steam," he said. "Next issue the op-ed editors have asked Will and Stephanie to contribute pieces on why the mascot should go and why it should stay. We're going to press again in three weeks."

"I thought they only let seniors work on the school paper."

"I do layout for the paper and yearbook. I've got the skills to pay the bills, as it were." The *Granger Gazette* and the yearbook shared an office down in the basement near the music rooms.

"Oh. Cool." How many extracurricular activities did this guy rack up? "I was wondering if you know where Stephanie is? I need to talk to her about something."

Fear flickered on his face. He looked like a squirrel in a dog's sights.

"Um, you know, I'm not sure," he said, obviously lying.

"Oh, okay. Well, if you see her, could you let her know I'm looking for her?"

"Sure thing!"

I knew he wouldn't mention it at all.

CHAPTER TEN

Sean hummed "Eye of the Tiger" the whole walk to the athletic center. The closer we got to the locker rooms, the louder his humming grew. "Cut it out," I said as he punched the air. "I'm already nervous."

"Nothing to be nervous about! So it's a big game. But in the grand scheme of things, in a world rife with famine, disease, war, natural disasters, and crime, is a game all that important?"

"Okay, now I'm nervous *and* feeling guilty for having First World problems. Thanks, bud," I said as we reached the hallway outside the locker room.

"Sorry. Just play like when we're at the park. Have fun with it! And if that doesn't work, pretend everyone watching in the stands and on the court is naked. Isn't that right, ladies?"

"Isn't what right?" Elle asked from behind me.

"Sneak attack from the back!"

"I did not see that coming, Kevin."

I turned around to find her and Erin in their gym clothes. Sweat trickled down the sides of their faces and their cheeks were flushed. Elle's practice jersey had a piece of black duct tape over the Gunner's rifle.

"Bijan's nervous about the game. It's like he thinks it's a big deal or something," Sean explained.

"I didn't think Bijan got nervous," Elle joked, walking a little bit closer to me. *Hummina hummina hummina.*

"It's been known to happen on occasion. Particularly when I make assumptions about comic book fans," I said. She smiled as she wiped her forehead with her wristband. "Will you two be watching?"

"It's our job to watch," Erin said. "We're taking pics for yearbook."

"Have a good game," Elle said. "I need good action shots, so no pressure. You'll be great." She and Erin walked to the girls' locker room, a place full of mystery, so close and yet so far away.

"Yeah. You'll be great," Sean said as he batted his eyelashes in jest.

"Thanks a lot." I gave him the finger, took a deep breath, and pushed open the locker room door to join my team.

"Balls to the wall, man! Show them what you got!" Sean yelled after me.

DJ Mustard's beats blared from the speaker Todd kept in his locker, meant to hype up everyone for the battle ahead. We were playing Armstead Academy, the jewel of the New England private day schools. Armstead had been ranked higher than Granger in some national magazine a few years earlier and officially became the school with the best facilities, the best teachers, and the most Ivy League acceptance letters.

Granger became the Kevin Love to Armstead Academy's LeBron James: an excellent choice, but not the ultimate choice. Granger games against Armstead always got the highest fan turnouts, particularly from alumni, even though we usually lost.

"Whose house is this?" Marcus yelled as he stripped off his shirt.

"OUR HOUSE!" the rest of us shouted back.

"I can't hear you! Whose house is this?" Will shouted, even louder.

"OUR HOUSE!" It felt kind of good to scream. I wished it were socially acceptable to scream more often. Not in class or anything, but maybe there could be some roped-off area on campus designated for screaming your cares away.

"What do we do to intruders?" Marcus yelled. I didn't know the response.

"CRUSH 'EM!"

"What do we do?" Will shouted.

"CRUSH 'EM!" I screamed with my team.

"When do we do it?"

"NOW!"

"When do we do it?"

"NOW!"

"Let's do it, then!" Marcus shouted as the team clapped and cheered.

"Yo, Will, we're going to hang at your place after?" Steve asked.

"Naw. Jessica's coming over tonight to like talk about feelings or bake cookies or whatever the hell will get her off my case about spending more time together," Will said, taking off his HERE TO STAY shirt. "I don't think she gets that, like, we're having fun, you know? Once I get what I need from her, I'm calling it off. Then it's college honeys for days, you know what I'm saying?"

Steve nodded, but nobody else seemed to care much about Will's love life.

"Hey, B. Good to see you," Will said as he put on his jersey.

"Always a pleasure, Will," I replied. The sarcasm in our words was thicker than the stench of the Axe body spray Steve layered on before and after a game. I turned to face my locker. Something smelled funky, probably Todd's socks—or maybe Will had crop-dusted farts.

"It's really nice of you to keep defending Busted Bergner. You giving it to her, man?" Will dry-humped the air. "I mean, I guess she'd be a good lay. She's got a nice physique for a munchkin. But all that talking, blah blah this, jibber jabber that . . . I'd be so distracted, you know? Such a boner killer."

I kept my back to him. I knew he wanted me to react. I knew he wanted me off the team and out of Granger. If I got into another fight, it would seem like I was the problem. I pretended to ignore him and struggled with my locker door, which was stuck.

"You put a bag over her head when you do her? So you can shut her up and not have to look at her? I know you people like your girls covered."

"Shut up, Will," Marcus said. "Why do you have to start stuff?"

"I didn't start anything! He's the one who put the school on edge. Can't say anything anymore without someone going all PC on you," Will countered. "Right, Drew?"

"Leave me out of it," Drew said. I watched him out of the corner of my eye. He was tying his shoelaces on the bench. But Will wasn't going to leave any of us out of it.

"Yo, Drew. I bet you'd screw Busted Bergner if she had a bag over her head."

Drew didn't respond.

"I bet you would. Lord knows Erin's not giving you any," Will continued.

I turned around to size Will up. I clenched my fists so hard, if I had been holding a walnut, I would have cracked it. I should have let him keep talking and left him alone, but I couldn't help myself. "Why don't you find a Jacuzzi jet to stick your dick into and call it a day, Will," I suggested.

Todd and Marcus laughed mightily at that one. Drew didn't look up, but I could see a slight smile on his face.

Will didn't seem at all embarrassed. He crossed his arms and puffed out his chest. I turned back around to try to open my locker again. I finally jerked the door with full force. It banged open.

My locker was stuffed with raw bacon. A giant mound of oily, slimy fat and protein lay on top of my practice pinnie and shorts.

"You get something from your secret psych?" Will asked. I slammed the door shut, grateful that my game uniform was in my gym bag.

"Come on, guys. Game's starting soon," Will said. I heard the shuffling of sneakers as some of my "teammates" exited the locker room.

"That's messed up," Todd said to me as I turned around. "Do you need help, uh . . . cleaning?" It was nice to know there was some shred of decency left in the wide world of Granger sports.

"I'd leave it there," Marcus said, his jaw tight with anger. "Let it stink the whole place up. Then Coach can't ignore it."

"We'll see you out on the court," Drew offered. It wasn't an apology, or even a kindness, but it was something. Recognition that I was a part of the group, even if he wished I weren't.

After the rest of the guys left, I sat down on the bench and slammed my fist down on the metal. I breathed heavily. The rage inside needed a place to go, needed someone or something to fight against without getting me kicked out of Granger. Armstead wouldn't know what hit them.

* * *

We were down by ten in the second quarter. My legs were bouncing up and down as I sat on the edge of the bench. I hadn't played yet, but I was fired up and ready to go.

I ignored the crowd, not bothering to check whether Elle was snapping photos for yearbook or Sean was sitting with my mom. I blocked out Coach's pep talks. I didn't cheer when our hands were in the huddle, though Coach didn't seem to notice. He had no clue what had happened in the locker room.

"B! You're in," he said after Drew got a reaching foul.

That was all the go-ahead I needed. I popped up like a jack-in-the-box and jogged over.

"Sub in for Drew."

I pointed to Drew, letting him know I was coming in for him. He looked at Coach in disbelief and jogged off. We didn't slap hands when we switched places. Didn't seem to be a point.

The Armstead player who was guarding me was a little shorter than I was, but a good defender. Poor guy. I was about to serve him his ass on a platter with a raw bacon garnish.

"And in comes Majidi with a chip on his shoulder. He breaks away from his defender like a streak of hot sauce across a chicken wing. Silva feeds him the rock. Majidi takes it to the hoop, and oh my, does he have hops! Look at how high he got, Reggie!"

"That's an easy two for the Granger Gunners. I feel like we're going to be seeing a lot of that tonight, Kevin."

I hustled back on D. Armstead's shooting guard launched a brick that I easily rebounded. I swung my elbows back and forth to let everyone know they had better get the hell away from me. They got the message loud and clear and backed off to their end of the court. I snapped the ball to Marcus, who put two fingers in the air to call a play.

Will didn't set a pick for me like he was supposed to. Coach noticed and shouted at him. Instead of waiting, Marcus threw the ball to Steve, who was open, but Steve wasn't ready for it. It sailed past him out of bounds.

"What the hell are you doing out there?" Coach screamed.

The guy I was guarding got hold of the ball, but I didn't let him breathe. I stayed on him, watching his stomach so I wouldn't fall for any ball fakes. He eventually got a pass off, but it was so telegraphed and desperate that Marcus was able to intercept, and he took it to the hole for two points. Armstead got the ball back but couldn't get a shot off before halftime.

Wiping sweat off my face with my jersey collar, I headed into the locker room. I expected to be met by the smell of funky spoiled bacon, but it smelled fine. We all found seats on the benches and guzzled down the water our team manager handed around.

"I don't know how many times I have to tell you guys to box out." Coach stood with his arms akimbo. "We are getting killed on offensive boards, and we can't win without second-chance opportunities! You know this! We've done the drills, we've talked about it all season."

Will made a point of sitting across from me to stare me down.

I stared right back.

"Earth to B and Thompson! You plan on paying attention, or you just going to make eyes at each other all night?" Coach yelled. Will finally looked away. I didn't look up at Coach. I kept glaring at Will, letting him know I wasn't going to be intimidated. "Why didn't you set that pick, Thompson? What's going on? We haven't had enough problems this week?"

The locker room was silent. No one was going to explain what had happened before the game.

"You all think I've got time for your petty crap? This is

the team now! Whether you like it or not . . . as a matter of fact, I don't care if you don't like it," Coach continued. "You're the team I've got. This is it. I'm going to play you till the end of our season, and if you don't like your teammates, if you don't like how much playing time you're getting, tough! We have a chance to beat Armstead. Granger hasn't done that in years. If you want to end the season early, that's up to you. If you're going to keep this up, we might as well call it a day. So either someone tells me what's going on or we can end the season right here and now."

"Something was left in Beej's locker," Todd said. I was surprised, but there was a reason he was cocaptain with Marcus. There was also a reason Will wasn't, and hadn't been a captain during his original senior year. The team stayed quiet. Steve looked at the floor, avoiding eye contact with everyone. Will's jaw clenched as he glared at Todd.

"Open it up, son," Coach Johnson ordered me.

I stood and opened my locker. Nothing was in there. There was no trace of the bacon or my practice clothes.

I spun around to face Will. "When did you do it?"

His face was blank, and he shook his head as if he didn't know what was going on.

"Who helped you?"

"I don't know what he's talking about, Coach," Will said.

"The hell you don't!" Marcus said, his nostrils flared in disgust.

"Whose side are you on, Marcus?" Will asked. "We've been teammates for years and you take the new kid's word over mine?"

"We're teammates, so I tolerate you. That doesn't mean I like you. Besides, Drew and I've been carrying your deadweight for two years. All you do is shoot Js that you can't make."

"Carrying me? That's rich. There wouldn't even be an athletic program like ours without my family's contributions." He couldn't help himself.

"Everybody shut up!" Coach barked. "Unbelievable. I thought I had a team of young men, and what do I have? I have a bunch of whining crybabies. I should have us forfeit. Is that what you all want?" Nobody said anything, but we knew he was bluffing. He wanted to win. He wasn't going to trade in the playoffs for a lesson about bullying.

Coach walked over to Will and squatted down, getting right in his face.

"When the play calls for you to set a pick, you set a goddamn pick. Got it?"

Will gave a slight nod, but he didn't look scared. Why should he be? Will was a Thompson. He could get away with anything.

"You're not at Trinity yet, kid. You think I don't know people over there? Huh?" Will looked away, but Coach stayed right there. "You remember who you play for. When

I tell you to hustle, you hustle. When I tell you to rebound, you rebound. Hell, when I tell you to take a piss during basketball season, you take a piss. And when I tell you to set a pick for someone, you set a pick, whether they're black, brown, orange, purple, or rainbow."

I bristled. I hated that kind of thing. It was usually a phrase dropped by people adamantly trying to prove they weren't racist. Purple and rainbow people don't exist. If I saw a rainbow person on the court, I probably *would* care, and I would ask them if they needed medical assistance. Will continued to look at the floor, but his face turned a deep shade of crimson.

"We understand each other?" Coach asked. Will nodded, but Coach waited, hanging there with his nose not even an inch away from Will's. Finally, he stood and walked back to face all of us.

"Now, I don't know what was in B's locker. Frankly, I don't think I want to know. I do want to know if we are going to continue to have a problem." This time he looked at me. Like I was the problem. Like they hadn't had any team issues until I showed up. My presence was getting to be a distraction, and Coach looked at me like it was my fault Will and Drew and Steve hated me. "Good," Coach said. "Marcus, I want you to keep feeding the ball into the paint."

That was it. We were all supposed to forget it and focus on the game.

By the time I subbed in for Drew toward the end of the third quarter, I was ready to rip somebody apart. Marcus inbounded the ball to me.

"There goes Majidi, dribbling fast down the length of the court, and—OH MY GOODNESS! He drops the sledgehammer! Up high and down hard!"

"Are you kidding me? The boy can dunk? Where has he been hiding that all this time?"

The crowd went nuts, but I didn't care. I just wanted to make the other team hurt. I wanted *someone* to hurt. Armstead called a time-out in an attempt to kill our momentum.

I walked over to our bench. Marcus jumped on my back.

Coach Johnson shook me by my shoulders. "That's what I'm talking about!" he said, but his approval didn't mean much at that moment.

"You didn't tell us you could dunk!" Marcus yelled. I hoped he wouldn't expect me to do it on a regular basis. I had practiced in the park with Sean, but it wasn't something I could do on command.

When we left the huddle, Armstead had decided it would be in their best interest to double-team me. It wasn't. Putting two guards on me left Marcus to send an easy feed to Todd under the rim, and Steve got a shot off too. They stopped double-teaming me after that.

I made it a point to go for every rebound. I only let two get away. Every time I jumped up to grab the ball, the crowd cheered louder and louder.

When Marcus called the same play from the second quarter, Will set a pick for me. No matter what he thought of me, he was going to listen to Coach. I darted behind the three-point arc. Marcus passed to me. When I dribbled to the hoop, the tall dude guarding Todd came up to block me. I bounce-passed to Todd under the hoop, and he got another bucket.

"That's it! Keep feeding the ball inside the paint," Coach Johnson yelled as we ran back on defense.

When we were beating Armstead by twenty points, Coach pulled me out and replaced me with a disappointed Drew. The crowd stood to applaud me as I walked to the bench. I didn't look up to thank them. I sat on the bench, sweaty, sipped water, and waited for the game to end. We won, in part because of me, again, because I did what I was supposed to do. It didn't change anything.

CHAPTER ELEVEN

The Monday after the game, everyone at school was staring at me again, but instead of suspicious glances and droopy, pitying stares, I was getting nods of admiration, thumbs-ups, and smiles. Students crowded around Sean and me as we walked to morning assembly. Some slapped me on the back. Others pantomimed my dunking for their friends.

"What's, um . . . what's happening?" I asked Sean as we sat in our seats. He had kicked out Charlie, who was more than happy to sit in the back indefinitely. The teachers hadn't objected, considering my "situation."

"I think you're a popular jock now," Sean answered plainly. Cassie Johnson and Emily Kartheiser, who sat in front of me, turned around.

"You were amazing on Friday," Cassie said.

"We finally got Armstead!" Emily offered me a high five. "I have a cousin who goes there. She's insufferable and always brags about how *great* it is there. I loved rubbing the score in her face!"

"Thanks," I said, slapping her clammy hand. I didn't think popular girls had clammy hands.

"Give him some love," Sean said, taking hold of my wrist and lifting it. The girls cheered and laughed. I had walked into a parallel universe. They beamed at me before they turned back around. They had sat in front of me for years and had never initiated a conversation with me during assembly.

"So let me get this straight, Kevin. Bijan . . . is a cool kid?"

"The coolest of the cool. Subzero. The Iceman not only cometh, he has arrived, and it's going to be a chilly time at Granger. Have your snowshoes ready and tell those dogs to mush, because Bijan is bringing on the FREEZE!"

* * *

"I don't get where the bacon went," I told Sean at lunchtime. Two sophomores fist-bumped me as they walked by our table. "I mean, my locker had to have been cleaned out during the first half." I looked down at my grilled cheese on my black plastic tray. Normally, I would have scarfed down two with tomato soup. But since the email, I wasn't eating a whole lot or paying much attention to my appetite. My mom had noticed.

I hadn't told her about the locker. I didn't want to add to her worries—or have her add bacon to the list of things to talk about at her stupid meeting the next week. Meanwhile, she kept cooking my favorite meals, even though she really didn't have the time. I would tell her I had a lot of homework to do, put my leftover food in Tupperware for the next day, then go to my room and lie on my bed, reading Gotham Central trades and trying to figure out who had sent that email.

"Maybe it wasn't someone from the team," Sean said around a mouthful of sandwich. "Will has a lot of friends in low places. I'm sure he could get some freshman to do his bidding."

It made my stomach churn to think there was a whole group conspiring to make sure I had a lousy junior year. I took in classmates' faces as they came and went, asking myself what I knew about them, whether I had said something to offend them, whether there was some reason they held a grudge against me. I was looking at everyone, hating that I was so paranoid. A few senior guys walked from the hot food bar and gave me the bro nod. I thought I remembered some of them wearing the HERE TO STAY shirts on Friday, but everybody loves a winner.

Behind the seniors, I spotted Stephanie and Noah holding their trays, looking for a place to sit because their usual spot was taken by freshmen. There was no seniority when it came to dorkdom. Stephanie noticed me and walked over to our table.

"Is anyone sitting here?" she asked us.

"You are," Sean said.

"Thank you." She sat down across from me, and Noah set his tray down next to hers. "How are you, Bijan? I was hoping we'd get a chance to speak."

"I was too." I wanted to talk to Stephanie, to apologize for the things I'd said and to ask her to leave me out of her mascot initiative, but not with Noah and Sean around. "Noah, did you tell Stephanie I was looking for her on Friday?"

Noah balked.

"No. He didn't," Stephanie said, her eyebrows knitted in confusion. "What did you want to discuss?"

"Maybe we'll find a time to talk about it later." I took a sip of water to avoid Noah's stare. His lips pursed. He looked at me like I was a fly on his windshield and he was about to turn on his wipers.

"Okay," Stephanie said, picking up on the uneasiness between Noah and me. "I wanted to let you know the board has agreed to listen to our position regarding the mascot at the meeting organized for the parents. Noah, Elle, and I are going to work on a presentation in the library tomorrow after school. If you'd like to continue to be involved, we'd love to have you work with us."

"Yeah, about that . . ." I said. A part of me couldn't believe she was still going through with this. She wouldn't even acknowledge that although she'd started this crusade, I was the one receiving the backlash.

"Hi!" Erin said, coming up to our table with Jessica in tow. "May we join you?"

"It's a free country," Sean said. "Until Jessica has her way with us."

"Har, har." Jessica waited for Erin to sit down next to Stephanie before she found a place at the table. I'm not even kidding. She was that allergic to us.

"What brings you over to our neck of the woods, Jessica?" Sean asked, finishing his drink with a long slurp. "Looking to broaden your horizons?"

Jessica scrunched up her face. There was that pinched look Sean had mentioned.

"We are here because Bijan played a great game and we wanted to congratulate him," Erin said.

"Uh, thanks." I didn't believe her, but maybe Sean was right. People love their sports stars, and athletics are the great social equalizer.

"I'm having a little get-together at my house after the game on Friday. I was wondering if you'd like to come," Erin said.

Three weeks earlier, I would have leapt at the chance to go to one of Erin Wheeler's parties. But at that moment, I couldn't think of a reason why I should say yes.

"It's nice of you to invite me, but I don't know if I'd mesh well with some of your guests," I said, looking at Jessica. Her boyfriend was first on my list of people who couldn't stand me. I could swear I saw her smirk. She knew

124

what had happened in the locker room. I bet Will told her all about it. I bet Erin knew too.

"We're not all like that," Erin said. "Plus, Marcus and Todd won't let you sit a party out."

"Could he bring a friend?" Sean asked, waggling his eyebrows.

"It's a pretty small gathering," Jessica said.

"You're all invited," Erin said. Stephanie squirmed a little in her seat. She was probably still deodorizing the shoes Drew had puked on at the last party.

"Okay. Thanks. I'll think about it." I half smiled at Erin.

"Are you ready to go now?" Jessica asked.

Erin turned to her redheaded minion. "I think I'm going to sit here for lunch."

Jessica snorted as she got up and went to go find people on her level.

"Was Jessica at the game, by any chance?" I asked as Erin helped herself to one of Stephanie's fries.

"She showed up at the second half. She didn't have her camera with her, so she wasn't really a great help for yearbook. Why?" Erin asked.

"Just curious." Jessica could have been the one to clean my locker out, but I had no proof. I almost asked Erin if Jessica had smelled like bacon that night.

"Should we bring anything? Champagne? Caviar?" Sean asked our exalted table guest and future hostess.

"Nah, I'll send Jeeves to go get some," Erin said.

"Seriously?" Sean asked.

"No," Erin said, giggling. "Just bring yourselves." Next to Erin, Stephanie finally relaxed. She didn't object when Erin took another fry.

"Erin Wheeler's got jokes! Who knew?" Sean commented. Not me. I didn't know much of anything anymore.

"Is Elle going to be there?" I asked.

Erin put her chin in her hand and batted her eyelashes at me. "Why don't you ask her?"

"Wait," said Noah. "You like Elle?"

"You obviously haven't been paying attention," Erin said. "To anything other than Stephanie's mascot thing, anyway." Noah's eyes widened. Stephanie cleared her throat and gave Erin a sharp look. Erin grabbed another fry off Stephanie's plate and bit into it. Hard.

"Why?" I asked Noah.

"Nothing. I thought—nothing." Noah shook his head. His eyes darted to Stephanie before he looked down at his plate.

He thought something was going on between Stephanie and me? Seriously?

CHAPTER TWELVE

"Now, when I'm yelling at you guys to box out, that doesn't mean this." Coach turned stiffly around on the court, jerking his arms and legs as though he were a robot. "It doesn't mean turn around, stare up at the basket, and wait for someone taller to get the ball."

I had changed into my practice clothes in the bathroom of the schoolhouse instead of in the locker room. Was it a chicken move? Sure. But I was all about self-preservation. I didn't want to deal with more surprises or fights in the locker room, so I avoided it altogether.

"When you box out, you have to initiate contact with your man," Coach said. He stood in front of Drew and put a hand on Drew's chest, craning his neck to address the rest of us. "So when I want to put my body between him and the ball, I've got to make sure I have a handle on him, and then maneuver in front of him." Coach quickly slid his foot to the side and pushed his butt in front of Drew's junk.

"This is fundamental stuff. You should have been trained to do this in middle school. This is basic basketball. The only guy to make a difference on the boards last game was B," Coach said. He waved me over to join them in the middle of the key.

"You know why he kept getting rebounds?" Coach asked the team.

Nobody answered.

"Because he was *always* moving. When a shot went up from our side, or from their side, he chased down the ball. He moved to the hoop. He didn't stare up at the basket with his mouth wide open catching flies, waiting to see if the shot went in." That last bit was directed at Will. I can't lie, I was glad Coach called him out on it, even if it wasn't a direct hit.

"So this next drill is in honor of your abysmal rebounding. The offensive man is trying to get possession of the ball at the top of the key without fouling. The defender tries to keep him away by boxing out. I count to four. Whoever doesn't meet their objective goes to the back of the line and does five push-ups. Whoever retrieves the ball faces off with the next person in line. Drew and B, you two start us off. Everyone else, line up behind them."

I got in my defensive stance, low to the ground with my hand in Drew's face. He was low too, on the balls of his feet, ready to pounce.

"I want to see quick feet and clean contact. No bowling each other over, just good defense," Coach said. He blew the whistle.

Drew was fast, evading me easily. He got to the ball within three seconds. I jogged to the back of the line and did my five push-ups. Drew then beat Todd, Steve, and Marcus to the ball, so I was in good company. Drew was on a mission.

Will thought the exercise was a wrestling drill. He yanked on Drew's arm and held it. Coach blew the whistle.

"Ten push-ups, Thompson. I told you not to foul," Coach said.

"I barely touched him," Will protested as he retreated to the back of the line and dropped to the gym floor.

"That's some Bill Laimbeer style of play right there. Rough, tough, and no sense of culpability for his actions, Reggie."

"Are you kidding me? Thompson wishes he had a career like Laimbeer's! Thompson has no grit. He crumples in a game like a paper napkin at a barbecue."

It was my turn again. The whistle blared. This time, I kept my hands behind me when I slid in front of Drew, keeping track of him and feeling his resistance against my back. We both ended up on the floor, scrambling for the ball, each of us grabbing it and playing tug-of-war. Coach blew the whistle and we stopped pulling, but neither of us let go.

"That's the kind of tenacity I want to see." Coach pointed at us. Apparently, we were a shining example for our teammates as we lay on the court like cats fighting over a ball of yarn. "Do it again."

Neither of us let go of the ball.

"It's a tie, you dopes. Get up. Try again," Coach said.

"Let go, man," Drew muttered as he gave the ball a jerk.

"You let go first," I said, tugging back.

"You!"

"Why me?"

Marcus and the other guys started to laugh at us. Coach blew his whistle.

"Are you two serious?" Marcus said, trying to catch his breath, before busting into another fit of laughter. "Acting like kindergartners! At least kindergartners are cute."

Drew and I looked at each other and cracked up. We both let go of the ball and watched it roll down the court. Drew got up first and offered me his hand. I took it. Then we ran the drill again. He beat me to the ball but lost to Todd right after me. I watched him do his push-ups at the back of the line. He did fifteen.

* * *

After practice, I killed time on the court shooting hoops to give Will and his pals time to change and leave before I showered. It was quiet, the lights were still on, but no one else was on the court or using the running track up above.

"Hey," I heard. I turned my head to find Drew, dressed in his varsity jacket and jeans, his sports bag slung over his shoulder.

"Hey." I stopped dribbling and held the ball in my hands.

"Did Coach hold you back or something?"

"No. I'm just shooting around," I said. He could rest easy. There was no secret plot for me to take over his position.

"Oh." I expected him to leave after that, but I guess he couldn't help himself. "I didn't have anything to do with the, uh . . . the locker thing."

"Okay," I said.

"No, really, I'm not . . . I don't want any problems with you. I've got enough to deal with." He wanted to make sure his ass was covered.

"Do you know who did it? *Any* of it?" I asked.

He didn't say anything. He had some idea, I knew he did, but he wasn't going to tell me.

"Whatever. Forget I asked."

"I honestly don't know who sent that email." I heard his sneakers squeak onto the court. "But I do know that I hate that Coach and Headmaster Clarkson think I might have done it. I've been in their offices more this past week than my whole time here. Did you say you thought it was me?"

"Trust me, your name never left my mouth. But they're not stupid. Everyone knows you're not my biggest fan." I turned away from him and bounced the ball before I took a shot. I laid a big fat brick against the rim. It bounced up high. I followed it, dribbling back to where I had last shot.

"Why don't you quit?" he asked. I turned around to look at him. There wasn't a hint of malice in his voice or on his face. He was genuinely curious. "I mean, why not wait for all this stuff to die down? Coach will have you be a starter next season when all the seniors leave."

I could have quit. It would have been easy enough. They needed me. I would have loved to see Coach Johnson beg me to stay on the team.

"I shouldn't have to quit something I love. Would you quit?"

Drew blinked at me. "I don't have the option. Granger uses me to win basketball games, and I use Granger to get to college. That's the deal."

I didn't exactly feel heartbroken for the guy. Whatever he felt about the game, he still acted like an ass, but it hadn't occurred to me that being on the team was a job for him.

"I'm not quitting," I said. I was stating a fact for him, and for myself. He put his bag down and raised his hands for the ball. I sent him a hard chest pass. He squared up, dribbled twice, and made his shot. The splash echoed throughout the gym. He held his follow-through arm in the air for me to make sure I got a good look at it, to let me know he was the best one on the court.

"Fine. Don't quit. But I wasn't involved with any of that stuff that happened to you. Did I want to punch your face for interfering with my girl and me? Yeah. But my beef with you is on the court and that's it. Got it?"

"Not very sportsmanlike, Reggie. Not at all."

"That's true, but there's nothing like a little competition to rev up a player's game."

"Sure. I got it." I didn't go after the ball. He backed away and picked up his bag, turning toward the door. "But I heard she's not your girl anymore."

"Oooooh! Anyone got Icy Hot for that burn?"

"Stings so good, Kevin!"

I expected him to get angry and try to fight me again. Instead, his shoulders slumped and his neck sagged. "Working on that." The poor sap really thought Erin Wheeler was going to take him back. "Will and the guys left already," he said as he walked out of the gym.

I scooped up the ball and dribbled to the spot Drew had made his perfect shot from. I missed. I kept shooting until I made it.

CHAPTER THIRTEEN

I headed to the library for a moment alone with Stephanie to clear the air before the mascot meeting started.

Posters that had the Gunners logo crossed out with a giant red X seemed to be popping up everywhere. Flyers were taped up in the cafeteria. Larger posters were placed next to the black-and-white photos of previous headmasters that hung in the schoolhouse hallways. Ms. McCrea had put one up in her classroom.

I had mixed feelings about it. Part of me couldn't stand the mascot anymore. It kept reminding me of the stupid email. We could have a giant octopus named Ollie, for all I cared. Maybe then I'd start to feel a little better. But I also didn't like that pro-Gunner students were wearing their HERE TO STAY shirts more often.

I entered the way-too-hot library and loosened my tie.

Ms. Spooner was whispering to a kid at the front desk about a book he was checking out. The couches up front were occupied by students reading their paperbacks of Hemingway and Faulkner with highlighters in hand.

Elle was sitting by herself at one of the tables toward the back when she saw me. I waved to her and walked over.

"Hey," she said. "Do you know if the meeting is still happening? Stephanie and Noah haven't shown up yet."

"Oh. That's weird. They're usually so punctual."

"And inseparable. Or at least, it feels like Noah *wants* them to be." Elle closed her notebook and put it in her backpack.

"You noticed that too?" I dropped my voice to a whisper. "It's kind of creepy."

"I would hate having someone be a constant shadow like that. But that's her business, I guess."

"May I keep you company before you guys get going?" I shifted my weight from foot to foot.

"You're not staying for the meeting?" she asked, gesturing for me to sit in the chair across from her.

I sat down. "Uh, no. I hadn't planned on it."

"Oh." She sounded disappointed.

"I have a lot going on with school and the team." It wasn't a lie, but it wasn't the whole truth either. I couldn't tell her I had only volunteered to get signatures because I wanted an excuse to hang around her.

"Okay," she said. She didn't push me to explain.

"To be honest, I kind of wish I hadn't gotten involved," I said. "Sorry. I'm not as brave as you and Stephanie are."

"Maybe not," Elle said gently. "But I think you're as brave as you need to be right now."

I swallowed. That warm, gooey marshmallow feeling in my chest was back again.

"Are you okay?"

"What?"

"Well, you're sweating a lot, and you got pink all of a sudden," she said. She reached up to check my pulse under my neck with her fingers. Her worried expression slowly turned into a grin.

I laughed so hard. Maybe I still wasn't great at talking to Elle, but I had come a long way since that sophomore dance.

"Are you going to Erin's party?" I asked. She removed her fingers from my throat.

"I'm still on the fence. There are some people who will be there whom I'm not sure I want to spend time with anymore. Why?"

"I was thinking of making an appearance. It was either that or crash a birthday party at Chuck E. Cheese's. I hear they have top-notch sheet cake, a show, the works."

She played along. "I do recall they had pretty good pizza at Chuck E. Cheese's. Though I haven't frequented that establishment in quite some time."

"Same. I haven't been since last Saturday," I joked.

"Do they still have those animatronic robot characters? They were kind of freaky."

"You're right. They were terrifying. I promise never to bring the place up again." I crossed my heart. "I'm sure Erin and Jessica will be disappointed if you're not at the party."

"I think Jessica will be thrilled to have Erin all to herself," Elle said.

"I thought you were all tight?" I wasn't sure how cliques worked. I had never been a part of one.

"Erin and I are. Jessica and Erin are. Jessica and me, not so much," she answered. "Erin and Jessica were best friends at their old private school. When they got here freshman year, Erin and I clicked, but Jessica and I never really did. We like each other well enough, but we rarely hang out together without Erin. I think Jessica feels out of the loop since Erin's been kind of secretive lately . . ." I didn't think Elle knew who was providing Erin's tutoring sessions. She hesitated before saying more.

"Well, it's their loss if you don't go. And mine."

"What a cornball."

"I think it's sweet, Reggie."

"He has more corn than the Iowa State Fair."

"I'll think about it," Elle said. "Though you may need to sell me more on this Chuck E. Cheese's trip."

"I'll try my best," I said with a smile. "So—"

Noah barged between us, rushing from the back of the library toward the door.

"Noah, where's the fire?" I called as he blew past. He stopped for a moment and looked at us like he was the kid from *The Sixth Sense* seeing dead people for the first time.

"Hey, are we still meeting?" Elle asked.

He stared straight through her with glassy eyes. He didn't speak.

"Are you okay?" I asked.

He turned to me. His eyes bugged out of his face, and when he opened his mouth to speak, he gnashed his teeth. "Did you know?" His lips contorted. He looked like a guard dog snarling at a trespasser.

"Know what?" I asked. I stood up, placing myself between Elle and him. When he realized I didn't know what he was talking about, he left the building in a huff, pushing the double glass doors of the library open. Ms. Spooner called after him, upset that he'd made so much noise in her domain.

"What on earth is wrong with him?" Elle whispered.

"I'm not sure."

"I better get to practice." Elle put on her coat. "I'll text you if I end up at Erin's."

"Really?"

She pulled out her phone and gave it to me so I could enter my number. I think my hand trembled. I felt like a college kid who'd just been told he was about to be drafted to the NBA. I gave her phone back.

"See you later, Bijan," she said as she pocketed it. I

watched her walk outside, zipping up her coat to brace herself against the bitter cold. Watching her go, I knew I wanted to be her favorite person someday.

The sound of giggling nearby snapped me out of my Elle haze. Erin exited one of the study rooms. Stephanie followed close behind.

"Hey, Stephanie," I said. They both whipped around to face me.

Stephanie looked anxious, but Erin kept grinning. "Hi, Bijan."

"What's up?" Stephanie asked.

"I wanted to talk to you before your meeting. We left things kind of . . . um . . . I wanted to squash the weird."

Stephanie's eyes grew large and she put her hand to her forehead.

"The meeting! I'm late! I completely lost track of time," she said. Stephanie Bergner lost track of time? Didn't she have a spreadsheet for every occasion?

"I don't think the meeting's happening anymore," I told her. Stephanie blinked and waited for an explanation. "I was talking to Elle while she was waiting for you, but she had to go to practice. Then Noah ran by us from the back of the library, all freaked out, and he stormed out of the building."

Stephanie blanched, but Erin mostly maintained her composure, aside from her eyes darting side to side.

"I didn't notice him," Stephanie whispered.

"I didn't either," Erin said with a twinge of concern in her voice. "Did he say anything?"

"He asked me did I know, but he didn't elaborate. He looked like he was about to have a fit."

Stephanie started fiddling with the cuff of her shirt, picking at the button as though she was trying to tear it off.

Erin placed a hand over Stephanie's and looked into her eyes. "It's going to be fine," she promised.

Stephanie nodded, but Erin didn't take her hand away until Stephanie stopped fidgeting. "I'll wait for you in the parking lot. Okay?"

"Okay," Stephanie said. Erin took a deep breath and turned to me.

"Hope to see you both at the party," Erin said. She left us alone to roam the stacks.

"I shouldn't have been late." She was saying it to herself, *blaming* herself, as she took a seat next to me.

"I'm sure you can reschedule," I said, touching her shoulder. I watched her eyes flit back and forth.

"I think Noah may have seen something he shouldn't have," Stephanie said, more to herself than to me.

"I'd offer to beat him up for you, but that didn't work out so well last time." It was supposed to be a joke, but comedy is all about timing, and mine was way off.

"I didn't ask you to intervene!" Stephanie snapped. "That argument was between Drew and me."

"No, but you asked me to be involved with that petition, and look how that turned out. Then you gave an interview about me to the school paper without letting me know?"

"I thought they were going to make up, Reggie."

"We're going to need to tune in to Secaucus, New Jersey, for the instant replay."

Stephanie closed her eyes and took a deep breath. It was probably something she'd learned in her conflict resolution seminar.

"I am sorry about what happened to you," she began. "I meant what I said to the *Gazette*." I believed her. Stephanie Bergner was a lot of things, wore a lot of hats, but she wasn't one to lie. "But I did not create that image of you. Nor did I force you to help me. I asked, and you agreed."

She was right. When she called me to get signatures for the petition, I could have said no. Still, couldn't she just let it go? Her petition was doing way more harm than good.

"You think changing the mascot is going to make this place Candy Land? You think if we pick a badger or a leopard instead of a colonial soldier, the school is going to be a more tolerant place with fewer bullies?"

"Well, not if we pick a badger. That's not very compelling."

I didn't want to, but I chuckled.

"So something more compelling than a badger will create a more enlightened student body. Got it." I still wasn't buying it. "Why do you have to bring it up now, though?

I mean, junior year is almost over. We'll be out of here soon. Who cares what the school mascot is?"

Stephanie placed her hands flat on the table and looked at them for a moment. I didn't rush her.

"I have not had the easiest time at this school," she said. "I know what people say about me and post about me online. But I can take it. I don't like it, but I'm resilient enough to not let in get in my way. The Gunners logo, in my opinion, is a symbol of compliance. When the school supports the mascot instead of the students who are made uncomfortable by it, it means that the school feels those students should put up or shut up. The message is 'If you don't like it, go to somewhere else.' I don't want another present or future Granger student to feel they have to comply with the status quo when they don't feel comfortable doing so."

She felt more strongly about this than I'd given her credit for. Stephanie put so much energy behind so many causes that it felt almost impossible to believe she cared about all of them. But maybe she really did.

"I am sorry that I snapped at you the other day. I know the email isn't your fault," I said.

"But you wish you hadn't helped me out at the party or with Drew?"

"I don't know," I said. "But I do think we both could use all the friends we can get."

She nodded. My phone buzzed and I fished it out of my pocket. It was a text from a number I didn't recognize.

In case you want to talk. But not about Chuck E. Cheese robots. Maybe I'll see you at Erin's.

"Good news?"

"What?" I asked, looking up from my phone.

"You're smiling," Stephanie said.

"I think I'm going to go to Erin's party after all," I said, feeling a little cocky.

"Oh." Stephanie wriggled in her seat. "I haven't decided whether I'll attend."

"We were invited. By your tutee, the most popular girl in our grade, no less." I was playing with fire.

"Oh, is she?" Stephanie said, her voice oozing sarcasm. "I hadn't noticed."

"She might be upset if we don't go."

"She might be. There may, however, be some people who will be upset if we *do* go." She was right. My cyber-friend might be there. A lot of the people who were mascot traditionalists and called Stephanie "Busted Bergner" would probably be there too.

"So do we let them win by not showing up?"

Stephanie's lips curled into an almost-smile. She didn't say anything, but Stephanie Bergner hadn't run away from conflict since I'd known her. I didn't think she'd start now. Plus, I was finally a big man on campus. Why shouldn't I get to enjoy the perks that came with that?

CHAPTER FOURTEEN

"All hail the conquering hero!" Sean announced as he walked into Erin's house ahead of me. We had beaten St. Christopher's 54–32. Not to brag, but I was on fire! I scored eight points, made two assists, had one block, and got three rebounds. The win ensured our team a place in the New England tournament.

"It was a thing of beauty watching Bijan play tonight, Reggie. An unforgettable night."

"I don't think he's going to be in any State Farm commercials yet, but give him time!"

Erin greeted Sean, Stephanie, and me at the front door. We'd made it a point to show up together. I had convinced Stephanie that there was strength in numbers, and that splitting a ride three ways from school would cut our Lyft fare considerably. The plan for the ride home was to drop Stephanie off at her house first; Sean would sleep over at my place. Stephanie hadn't heard from Noah, nor had he offered her his chauffeur services. She seemed upset when she told us he hadn't answered any of her calls, but I didn't ask her about it. Their friendship was her business. I did, however, make sure she didn't have a clipboard with her.

"Hey, you made it!" Erin found us in the foyer. "Hi, Steph." Not Stephanie, not Bergner, but Steph.

"Hello, Erin," Stephanie said, looking at her momentarily before averting her eyes and blushing a little.

"Phones and car keys, please." Erin held up an orange beach pail three-quarters filled with brightly colored phones and keys. We emptied the contents of our pockets and paid the fee.

"Why no phones?" I asked.

"No phones, no incriminating photographs of underage drinking. Makes for a more relaxed evening. Good game, by the way. Elle got lots of great shots for the yearbook."

Yearbook! Action shots! The stuff of high school legend!

"Nice digs," Sean said. Erin's house was huge and full of New England old-money furniture, understated but expensive.

"We're all hanging out in the kitchen." Erin led us through her expansive house.

"Thank you for inviting us," Stephanie said.

"I'm glad you came," Erin said.

Drew, Marcus, and Todd sat at a round wooden table in the kitchen, Solo cups in hand. "There he is!" Marcus said, standing up to greet me.

Sean immediately went to hug him. "I *am* here! It's so good to see you." Sean stuck his hand up in the air for a high five from Drew, but Drew didn't go for it.

"Hey," I said as I slapped hands with Marcus.

"Your boy is crazy. You know that, right?" Marcus asked as Sean sat down with my teammates.

"What are we having, fellas?" Sean asked. He had glaze splatters on his khakis and a Deadpool sweatshirt on. He hadn't exactly dressed up for our big night out.

"Beer," Drew said before taking a sip from his Solo cup.

"Bread juice. Cool. I can wrap my head around that."

"It's in there." Todd pointed to the deluxe wood-paneled fridge.

"I'll come with you," I said, leaving my teammates behind. Stephanie sat with Erin on the barstools surrounding the granite-countertop island in the center of the kitchen.

"You guys want something?" Sean asked them. He opened the refrigerator and pulled out a craft Belgian. Erin had the fancy stuff!

"No, thank you," Stephanie answered as she watched Jessica and some of her field hockey teammates play Never

Have I Ever. Jessica was laughing loudly and looked like she'd had a few drinks already. A shot glass with a lime rind inside it lay on its side in front of her.

"I'll have one," I said. If I held a beer for a while, no one would ask me why I wasn't drinking. Pretending to nurse a beer all night couldn't hurt. Plus, Mom would be happy that I was socializing and not moping around the homestead.

Sean passed me a bottle. Maybe I'd even drink some. Why not? I was at Erin Wheeler's mansion after a big win. Shouldn't I celebrate like everybody else?

* * *

After an hour, Sean was three beers in and dancing with some field hockey girls. Maybe that would have been a good time to start drinking in earnest. I had nursed my one beer, but it tasted like wheat backwash. I didn't see why people liked it so much.

"No, you're funny!" Sean cooed to one of them.

"Nooo . . . *you* are," she said, bopping him lightly on the nose.

That girl probably wouldn't even say hi to him in the hallway on Monday, let alone laugh at one of his jokes with her friends around. She bopped his nose again and Sean pulled her closer. I tore my attention away and stared at one of Erin's parents' many pieces of art instead. Sean was always at ease with himself, whereas I couldn't quite figure out how to get out of my own way. He wouldn't have even been invited to the party if it weren't for me, but here he was, having a great time, while I pretended to like my lukewarm beer.

I looked around for Stephanie and found her in conversation with a few juniors. She didn't seem to be in any distress. The music was blaring, and I swayed back and forth, hoping no one would notice I had no rhythm.

"I didn't know you could dance," Elle said beside me. I immediately remembered why I'd come to this party. I straightened up and smiled at her.

"I can't," I promised. "This is about the extent of my dancing."

"Your new friends don't seem to mind," she said, nodding in the direction of the girls grinding with Sean.

"Those are Sean's friends. I'm more particular about my dance partners." I stepped closer to Elle.

"I didn't know you could flirt either."

"That's the alcohol. It convinces me that I can."

"Oh. I didn't know you, um . . . I thought you weren't supposed to drink?"

"Well, yeah, my mom would freak out, but I figure when in Rome, right?"

"Sorry, I thought, um, because you're . . . Never mind," she said.

I suddenly understood what she meant. I looked at the

beer in my hands but didn't say anything about it. "So where are Erin's parents?"

Elle paused and blinked the way Stephanie usually did when something didn't compute or when she was caught off guard. Excuse me, the way *Steph* did.

"They're at a destination wedding this weekend," Elle said, both of us happy to change the subject from my drinking. "Though they aren't exactly home a lot. Erin's been my friend for years and I've only seen them a handful of times. She's not really close with them."

"Is she really close with anyone?" I asked, though I had a feeling I knew one person outside of the New Crew Erin was close with.

"She's guarded, but she lets people in if she trusts them. Not the people who suck up to her, but people she cares about and who care about her. We have that in common."

"Trust is important," I said, bouncing my shoulders up and down. She shook her head, unimpressed by my deep shoulder-action moves. "Do you think I'm trustworthy?" I really, really hoped she did.

"I haven't decided yet," she said. It wasn't a playful response. It was a vulnerable one, which meant she was interested enough to be honest.

"This feels like a great moment between Powell and Majidi, but I may be a little tipsy, Reggie."

"Woo! I'm feeling goooooood! Fired up and ready to party, Kevin!"

"Can I prove to you that I am? I can give you references. My mom thinks I'm fairly trustworthy. Aside from that time I lied about drawing in crayon on her bedroom wall. But to be fair, that was a while ago."

"How old were you? Three? Four?"

"It was last year, but I'm learning and growing every day."

"She's laughing, Reggie! This friendship could turn into romance after all! It is a thing of beauty watching these two open up to each other!"

"I don't care. Where's the tequila?"

"So what comics are you reading?" I asked her.

We talked about Daytripper, Ms. Marvel, She-Hulk, and Blacksad. We talked about her overachieving older siblings at university, whom she felt she had to live up to. I told her I had always wanted an older brother. We talked about what we hoped to study in college. She knew her parents wanted her to study law, but she wanted to pursue filmmaking and be a cinematographer. I told her about wanting to give sports broadcasting a try and how I hadn't told my mom because she'd hate it.

We talked about our favorite foods, the worst movie either of us had seen, which deceased musicians we wished we had seen in concert, if we could choose a superpower what we would choose and why. She chose flight so she could travel the world. I chose superspeed so I could be in two places at once if I needed to be. If there was any good thing that came out of subbing in for that varsity game, it was that Elle and I talked.

I was trying to come up with something that would make her laugh again, but then Drew rushed into the living room, chasing after Erin. "I want to talk some more," he pleaded. He was a little loud and a little drunk. Erin did an about-face and furiously whispered something to him, but he didn't back off.

"Hey, Erin," Elle called, and waved her over. "Can you come here real quick? I need to ask you something." Erin sighed with relief as she walked over to us. Drew followed, but Erin kept her back to him, excluding him from the conversation.

"Hey, you two," Erin said casually, with maybe a small catch in her voice. "Having fun?"

"So that's it? Just like that, you're done?" Drew leaned over her shoulder. Erin's face became red, but she didn't turn around to answer him.

"I have been done, Drew. We both said what we needed to say."

He put his hands on the top of his head the way he did when he was called for a foul. We briefly made eye contact, but he looked away. He skulked out of the living room.

"Coast is clear," Elle said. "Are you okay, Erin?"

"Fine. I thought I'd made it obvious to him last week, but guys can't take no for an answer," Erin said.

"Not all—"

"Don't finish that sentence," Elle said to me.

"Sorry," I said. I looked over Erin's shoulder and saw Stephanie staring at us.

"I should have called it off a while ago," Erin was explaining to Elle. "I feel bad. He likes me more than I like him, and it isn't working."

"You did the right thing," Elle replied. "You shouldn't keep a relationship going just because everyone expects you to."

"Yeah, but . . ." Erin began, but then she looked at me and stopped.

"Ooooh, and there is a delay of game."

"I'm going to let you two talk," I said. I smiled at Elle.

"Could you . . . I know this is going to sound dumb, but could you maybe check on him?" Erin asked me. "Or have one of the guys check on him? Make sure he isn't drinking too much?"

She wanted *me* to babysit Drew? "I don't think I'm the best candidate," I said, but Elle looked at me and I caved. "Okay, I'll take care of it. Maybe we can catch up later?"

"I'd like that," Elle said.

I meandered down the stairs to check out the basement. I was annoyed that Drew had killed my moment with Elle with his own crappy love life. A few kids congratulated me as I went by.

The basement rec room was a throwback to the sixties: shag carpeting, modern furniture, a small bar jutting out from the wall, and a Ping-Pong table. Drew sat by himself on a brown leather couch under a framed vintage travel poster of Tahiti. His not-so-sunny disposition really didn't go with the decor. This must have been Mr. Wheeler's man cave.

"What is Majidi doing, Kevin?"

"I think he's entering the danger zone, Reggie."

I took a seat on the other end of the couch, making sure there was plenty of space between us.

"You come to rub it in my face?" Drew asked, looking straight ahead instead of at me.

"No. Needed to find a place to sit. The field hockey girls took over the living room, so I thought I'd come down here," I lied.

"She sent you down here, didn't she?" Drew asked. He didn't have a drink in hand, which I took as a good sign. I didn't answer, but he nodded and leaned back into the couch. "Figures. She cares about me, but not enough to make it work."

I didn't know which clichéd phrase about love I could use to comfort him. "Plenty of fish in the sea" was too trite. "There's always another bus at the station" was dumb, because women aren't buses. Truthfully, I didn't know that I *wanted* to comfort him.

"Sean says there's an ass for every saddle. It's kind of crude, but he has a point." I rolled the corner of the label off my beer bottle with my thumb, reminding myself that

I was doing this for Elle. I was being nice to Drew Young for Elle.

Drew chuckled. Evidently he hadn't heard that one before.

"Where is your right-hand man, anyway?"

"Dancing with the field hockey team. He has no trouble finding saddles," I said, a little bitter. "You're not going to operate any heavy machinery anytime soon, are you?"

"Don't have a car and no one would lend one to me, so you can tell Erin not to worry," Drew said, rubbing the top of his head.

"I don't have a car either. Sucks," I said. "I mean, not that I am owed a car or anything, but most kids at Granger who can drive have cars."

"Most kids at Granger have lots of things," Drew said, waving his arms at our surroundings. I half expected the vintage jukebox in the corner of the room to start playing music on cue.

I heard thuds coming from the stairway. Marcus appeared, holding a tall stack of red Solo cups. "Hey! Where have you been, all-star?" he asked me as Todd followed him, holding a six-pack of Fat Tire beer.

I felt Drew sit up straight on the couch.

"Drew and I were talking about the game," I lied. "We want to make sure we're ready for the tournament."

Drew looked at me in confusion. Hey, I wasn't one to

kick a guy when he was down. My mom raised me better than that.

"You were on point tonight, man," Todd told me as he set up the cups on his side of the Ping-Pong table.

"We were all on point," I said.

"Even Will," Drew chimed in. His focus turned from me to Marcus, who was pouring beer into the cups. "Mostly because Coach finally sat his ass on the bench." We all laughed, but I knew Drew wouldn't have said that if Will were in the room.

"I think we can win the tourney," Todd said, picking up the Ping-Pong ball from the table and bouncing it once before catching it again.

"Yeah, but I'll be glad when the season is over," Marcus agreed. "I'd like to take a break and enjoy more of my senior year."

"College ball will be awesome," I promised Marcus. "Where are you going next year? I heard UConn was sweating you pretty hard."

"They were. I'm waiting to hear back from my first choice, though," Marcus responded. "MIT."

"But that's a D-Three school!" Why would he want to play for a Division III school when he could play Division I–level ball?

"You're starting to sound like Coach," Marcus replied. "MIT has an amazing civil and environmental engineering program. That's what I want to do, be a civil engineer."

Todd threw the Ping-Pong ball at one of Marcus's cups and missed.

"I never knew that!" I said a bit too eagerly.

"You never asked." Marcus was right. Apart from talking about basketball, I'd never really gotten to know him. In fact, I hadn't really gotten to know any of my teammates, or had much time to. "How about you, Beej? You want to play ball in college?"

"I don't know that I'm good enough."

"If you practice this summer with Coach and Drew, you'll be good enough," Marcus said as he aimed for one of Todd's brews. "I guarantee it." Drew and I sized each other up. Spend the summer one-on-one? "It'd be good for the both of you. Drew could help you get your game up, and maybe you could help Drew loosen up a little." Marcus shook his shoulders in Drew's direction as he released the ball in a beautiful arc. It plunked in Todd's cup.

"You'd only have to spend one summer of your only God-given young life with Coach," Todd said, fingering the ball out of the cup before downing his drink.

"He's tough. But I feel sorry for him sometimes," Marcus said. "He doesn't have any kind of life outside the team."

"I don't feel sorry for him when he's barking at us to do suicides," Todd said, turning his empty cup upside down.

"Yeah, but making you do suicides is all he's got," Marcus said. "He only teaches middle school civics because he has to teach something full-time in order to coach. He's got no family, no social life. Plus, can you imagine what it must be like to be demoted from coaching college ball to high school? Even if the high school is Granger? It's a total downgrade."

"Doesn't he have a daughter?" I asked. The guys didn't say anything. "He has a photo of her on his desk."

"She passed away," Drew said.

"I didn't know that," Todd said.

"Coach doesn't like to talk about her."

* * *

So beer pong wasn't my game. I played with the guys for an hour, until I had to relieve myself. I wobbled over to the too-long bathroom line. There was only one bathroom open to us guests. What were my options? Pee my pants or step outside and find a tree to autograph.

I went out the back door. The Wheelers' home was on a hill on what must have been an acre of old farmland in the suburb of Weston, with a small creek running across the bottom. I walked past a few kids smoking on the corner of the patio, where the pool was covered with a tarp for the season and a few patio chairs stacked up for the winter were covered in snow. I walked down the slope until I was far enough away that I couldn't hear any music from the party. I spotted a tiny toolshed tucked away by some snow-covered pine trees. It was far enough from the house that I felt comfortable taking a leak.

I walked to the back of the shed. I tried to pick which shrubbery planted near the side of the structure might benefit from some alternative methods of watering. I had already undone my fly when I overheard some not-so-quiet conversation coming from inside.

I zipped myself up and squatted behind a clump of bushes. I didn't want to get caught with my pants down in Erin Wheeler's backyard. That was when I heard Stephanie.

"I'm not going to demean myself and, what . . . make myself over to appease your insecurities," she hissed, her voice rising to a yell before she regained her composure. "We've been playing this game for months. What are we doing? Are you . . . are you into me or aren't you? These mixed signals no longer feel healthy. Because I . . . While we haven't done anything, I like you. I like you very much. Can you understand that?" She didn't say anything for a moment. When she did speak again, her voice trembled. "Please. I need you to understand that."

Then I heard it. Lips smacking. Stephanie was kissing someone! Either that or she was really enjoying a Popsicle in the dead of winter. Even though I was curious to know who else was in that shed, it was time for me to exit this private moment.

There was one problem. I heard a rustling coming from

a bush about fifteen feet away from me. A little kitty with white stripes on its back emerged, and we locked eyes.

The rest of me froze too. I didn't want to get caught eavesdropping, but I also didn't want the skunk to get scared and spray me. I thought the best course of action was to stay crouched down until the skunk scurried away, when I could give Stephanie all the privacy she needed.

"You said you liked me," I heard a voice say.

A girl's voice.

A very specific girl's voice.

"That's the first time you said it." There was no denying that husky voice belonged to Erin Wheeler.

"Was it the first time? I thought I'd already told you," Stephanie whispered, breathless.

I stared at the skunk in disbelief. My furry friend didn't seem to appreciate the enormity of what was happening inside the shed.

"I pay attention to everything you say. Which is not always easy, considering how verbose you are," Erin said.

Stephanie laughed. "You've been studying those SAT cards I gave you. What do we do now?"

"I don't know."

"Of course you don't. You finally admit your feelings for me, but only in private, right?"

"Look, I broke up with Drew—"

"So there's nothing holding us back anymore," Stephanie

interrupted. "I was never going to be the other woman to that Neanderthal." She paused. The skunk was sniffing a pinecone. My quads burned from crouching for so long. "Unless you don't want to let people know?"

"It's not the being out of the big gay closet part that bothers me. It's . . . My friends and that school are going to tear you apart."

"I don't think you give your friends enough credit. I've spent some time with Elle, and she hasn't been mean to me in the slightest." I could picture Stephanie crossing her arms. I could also picture her lecturing me for eons if she knew what I was up to at the moment, so I stayed as quiet as possible.

"Yeah, but . . . I don't want you to . . . deal with more junk than you usually do," Erin said. "Can we please table this whole out-and-proud business? We'll figure out what to do over the summer."

"Don't pretend that this is about protecting me. It's about protecting you and your social status." Stephanie no longer bothered to keep her voice low.

Meanwhile, the skunk was foraging through the snow. There was no way I was getting out of this without smelling like rotten eggs, and I still had to pee so *bad*.

"Can we at least kiss some more before we have to have everything figured out?" Erin asked. "In my room, maybe? It's freezing out here."

"I'd be amenable to that," Stephanie said, and I heard

Erin gasp. Stephanie Bergner had game, way more game than I did.

I was sitting on the most amazing secret of all time, and a locker room story for the ages about the skunk (who was still chilling way too close for comfort). But I wouldn't say anything, even to Stephanie, until she told me about it. I shouldn't have been there. But oh man, I'll always have the memory.

"That skunk doesn't look like it's going anywhere anytime soon, Reggie."

"Nope. Sure doesn't. It looks like Majidi has lots of time to work on toning his quads."

* * *

My new friend Fluffy and I stayed out in the cold well after Stephanie and Erin went back into the house. Just when I thought my situation was headed from bad to worse, he waddled back into the bushes. As soon as Fluffy was out of my sights, I stood up and relieved myself. After I finished, I booked it back to the house. I didn't want to take a chance on Fluffy's relatives stopping by.

As soon as I rushed inside, Will managed to find me and slapped me on the back. "Yo, there he is," he said. He was wearing his Granger warm-up pants and jacket, as though he was still waiting to be put in the game. "Having a good time, Beej?"

"I was," I said.

"Your boy Sean is having a blast upstairs," Will said. He leaned right in to my face, doing his best to intimidate me. "I thought you two were joined at the hip. How will you be able to take a piss without him holding your dick?"

"He's his own man," I said. "But it's true, my dick is far too big to hold. Your mom said so last night." I had never met Will's mom, but if I ever did, I would apologize to her profusely.

"By the way," Will retorted, "which of his moms did it with a turkey baster?"

I pushed Will away from me.

He just laughed, backing away with his hands up. "You think you're a big deal now?" He had a stupid grin on his face. "I got some friends at Mercer Day I want you to meet at the tourney next week. I've told them all about you, and they're real excited to meet you." He turned around and sauntered over to a sophomore girl. He put his arm around her waist and nibbled on her earlobe. I guessed he and Jessica were off again.

* * *

I looked for Sean. It didn't feel right to leave him alone after what Will had said. What if Will had done something to him while I was creeping on Stephanie and Erin? And *why* had I continued to listen in on them, anyway? Yeah, it was hot, and yeah, Fluffy was a problem, but that was a private moment.

I wandered into the kitchen to find Elle at the table with a group of seniors hanging on every word she said. Popular guys with nice cars who had no viral iconography casting a shadow over them and would never bring up Chuck E. Cheese's in her presence sat there rapt. I was kidding myself to think something could ever happen between us.

"Big fella's liquid courage has left the building."

"No party like a pity party, Kevin."

I left to scope out the living room, where I found Sean lying on the couch, snoring. A crude drawing of a penis graced his cheek. I licked my thumb and crouched down to rub some of the black marker off. Thankfully it wasn't Sharpie.

CHAPTER FIFTEEN

I woke up the next morning on my own living room floor to the sound of my mom banging pots and pans in the kitchen. Something was up; she never made breakfast. I usually had what she called "Cocoa Poops" because they were all sugar and terrible for my teeth. Her usual morning meal was coffee, sometimes paired with a banana.

Sean, lying next to me, had apparently rolled to the floor from the pullout bed. I had slept near him, in order to assist him as quietly as possible to the bathroom when he needed to hurl chunks, for his sake and for my mom's. After he puked, I helped him scrub the uninspired doodle from his face.

Sean lay on the couch barely awake, his hands covering his ears.

"How are you feeling?" I asked.

He grunted and turned over.

"Rise and shine, gentlemen!" Mom said with aggressive cheerfulness. She entered the living room with a cup of coffee in her hand. "Sean!" She stood over him. "Your moms are going to pick you up this afternoon. They assumed you wouldn't be ready to join them this morning."

"Whatever gave them that idea?" Sean mumbled into the carpet. "On a scale of one to ten, how upset did they sound?"

"I'd say nine and a half. But they're glad you made it home safe." My mom crouched to Sean's level. "Do you drink coffee?"

Sean shook his head, his face still buried in the carpet.

"Well, today is the day you start," Mom said, gently taking his hand and closing his fingers around the mug, which she had set beside him on the floor.

"Thank you, Dr. M," Sean said. "You have always been my favorite."

"And thank you for showing my son how awful a hangover is." She turned her attention to me. "Though I think he has some idea himself?"

"What? No way!" I lied. I hadn't put away beers like Sean had, but I worried she knew I'd had one. I had a feeling that later she was going to yell at me or punish me by taking me to her book club and having all the members ask me what college I planned on going to, over and over and over again.

"Fix the sofa, please," my mom said before she walked back to the kitchen. I held out my hands and pulled Sean up. We stripped off the sheets and folded the bed back into the sofa. Sean winced at the creak of the metal frame dropping into place.

"So how was the party?" Mom asked, once we had eased ourselves into chairs at the kitchen table. She kept her back to us as she chopped potatoes and onions for hash browns. Until then, I hadn't known slicing could be loud. "Any trouble last night?"

I didn't want to bring up my conversation with Will, and I definitely wasn't going to tell them about Stephanie and Erin. I shook my head. "It was fine."

"Not that I remember," Sean said, shrugging and gesturing to his scoured-clean cheek. "You should totally come to the next party, Dr. M."

"I *should* come next time to keep an eye on you, Sean," Mom said over her shoulder. She'd love that. Then she could watch me like the NSA monitors Verizon customers. "You're more than welcome to have get-togethers here. Without alcohol, of course." When the hash browns were done, she scrambled a few eggs in the pan and spread the cooked food across two plates. She sat at the table with us, sticking with her cup of coffee and banana in lieu of our heartier fare.

"I will let the ladies know," Sean said.

"The same ladies who left you to get wasted?" I muttered.

He didn't look up from his mug of coffee when he answered me. "My wingman left me to get wasted too."

I hadn't been the best friend to Sean lately. I had been so caught up in the team and my email problem that I hadn't really asked him much about what was going on with him. I knew he had an exhibition coming up for Granger Arts Night that he'd been working hard on in the ceramics studio, but I didn't know what day it was going to be or how it was going. I hadn't even asked if Granger had won the last JV game or if he'd heard back from that girl he liked who worked at the Central Square Starbucks.

"Sorry. I should have been looking out for you. I was kicking back with the guys from the team. Figured it wouldn't hurt to fit in a little better."

"By drinking?" my mom asked.

"You didn't drink in high school?"

"That's none of your business," my mom said. "But *you* are my business, and I am concerned about what's going on with you. You never drank before. I don't want you using alcohol to numb yourself."

"I was trying to have fun! What do you guys want from me? I'm sorry I don't meet your superhero criteria for dealing with narrow-mindedness, but what should I do? Go to that stupid board meeting? Be a poster child for the cyberbullied?"

Neither Sean nor my mom had an answer for me.

None of us ate very much at breakfast. Sean and I played video games in relative silence until Sean's parents picked him up. I let him pick the games.

* * *

After Sean left, I retreated to my room. Mom didn't yell or give me a speech about how disappointed she was; she left me alone to do homework. I was typing up an overdue essay for history class, but I was having a hard time focusing. Ms. McCrea had been understanding and given me extra time. I knew I had to get it done, but my thoughts wandered to the email, Elle, Stephanie swapping spit with Erin, Will's threats. Current events were making it almost impossible for me to focus on historical ones.

There was a knock at my door.

"I brought you a snack," Mom said, entering my room. She held a plate of grapes, apple slices, and fig jam on toast out to me, even though she knew I wasn't going to eat much of it.

"I'm not hungry," I said.

She placed the food on my desk next to my computer. "The Celtics are playing in an hour. I thought we could watch the game together?"

We used to watch the games together all the time when I was younger. I rocked a Kevin Garnett jersey while my mom complained that she wished I were a Lakers fan like her and her family. No matter what, she'd always let me watch the fourth quarter of playoff games, even if they went really late. But when Mom's workload became overwhelming, we didn't have time to watch together anymore.

"Maybe after I finish this paper," I said as I stared at my computer.

Mom didn't leave my room. Instead, she sat down on my bed. I kept my back to her. I didn't want her to lecture me about underage drinking or try to convince me to make a speech at the board meeting.

"When your father and I learned you were going to be a boy, we spent a lot of time thinking about a name for you," she said. "Your father thought of some names in Arabic that could be shortened, and I thought of some Persian ones to honor relatives. We considered a lot of English names too. We thought it would make your life easier in the long run for job interviews or roll call on the first day of school, that sort of thing. I had experience with that growing up here, but your father didn't."

My mom isn't one to wax nostalgic. She doesn't like talking about the past. I think it makes her too sad. I swiveled my chair to give her my full attention.

"Then we reminisced about when we met. When he found out I was Persian, he said if I was willing to go on a date with him, we would have a romance greater than that of Bijan and Manijeh from *Shahnameh*. I was embarrassed that I didn't know what he was referencing."

Mom flushed as she continued to tell the story of their first date: My father had a heavy accent and a wealth of knowledge in various areas, and he grinned at her every time she spoke. They asked each other lots of questions that evening. With each answer, Mom said she was more certain my father was the man she would marry. Just like that. Not love at first sight, but love at first meaningful conversation.

At the end of the night she asked him to tell her the story of Bijan and Manijeh. He was surprised she didn't know it. The story was a part of the great Persian poet Ferdowsi's epic poem *Shahnameh*, which roughly translates to *The Book of Kings*. It was written a thousand years ago and is twice the length of Homer's *Odyssey* and *Iliad* combined. I couldn't even make it through *The Odyssey* freshman year, so I kind of can't imagine reading this poem (especially if it wasn't going to be on a test).

Shahnameh helped keep the Persian language intact. The text used virtually no Arabic, in subtle protest of the Arab conquests of Iran in the seventh century. My mother asked if this offended my father. He answered that it didn't, but Ferdowsi would be appalled that an Arab knew more about his epic poem than a nice Persian girl.

My father told my mom that Bijan was a great Persian knight tasked with helping farmers whose crops were being attacked by wild boars. When Bijan traveled to enemy territory to vanquish the boars, he fell in love with a princess, Manijeh, who was the daughter of his country's greatest enemy.

"Your father always enjoyed stories where love comes out of hate. He was so ridiculously sentimental that way," she said softly. For a moment, and only a moment, she seemed to be back there, in that time and in that place. Then she cleared her throat, and it was gone. I don't know why she thinks she has to put on a brave face all the time, but maybe one day I'll be courageous enough, like the hero I was named for, to ask her.

"Do you have a nickname at school?" Mom asked with a hint of uneasiness. She knew Sean and the guys called me Beej sometimes, but she didn't know it didn't sit right with me when someone like Noah said it. Coach Johnson hadn't even *tried* to say my name. He might as well have called me by the number on my jersey. He probably wouldn't learn my name unless I made it to the NBA.

"Bijan suits me fine," I said.

"Good." She nodded. "Try to eat something, and let me know if you change your mind about the game." She gave me a wet smooch on my cheek, then left me to my work.

I swiveled back around in my chair, looked at my computer screen, and minimized my history paper. I opened up my Granger email to see what my English assignment was. There was a new email from another address I didn't recognize. It had been sent ten minutes earlier. I held my breath and braced myself. It was so stupid that little things like checking my email made me so anxious.

The subject read, "Granger's New 'It' Couple."

I hovered over the message for a moment. I didn't want whoever was sending these to have power over me. I didn't want them to break me.

An animated GIF appeared, but it didn't feature me. It was a black-and-white photo of Stephanie Bergner's face on a stick figure. Animated cartoon hearts replaced her eyes. Stephanie's stick figure was holding hands with one that had Erin Wheeler's face. Every few seconds, Erin's mouth opened and a rainbow streamed out of it.

The photoshop quality was haphazard. The caption underneath read, "#GrangerGays and #ComeOutCome OutLesbianSquashStar."

I waited a minute before I called Stephanie. She picked up immediately.

"I saw it," she said, her voice shaking with barely contained fury. "Erin's not picking up her phone, but I texted her. I don't know if she's seen it yet."

"I'm so sorry, Stephanie."

"My father . . . he's trying to get hold of someone on the faculty. Oh God! Erin's parents! She hasn't told them about—I mean, they don't know."

"Do you recognize the photo? Where it came from?" I asked. "The one of you, is it from the directory or Instagram?"

"No. I don't . . ." she said, breathing heavily. "I mean, I don't really post much of anything."

"Could it be a yearbook photo, maybe, or from the *Gaz*—" I stopped.

I do layout for them.

I've got the skills to pay the bills.

Did you know?

"I think I know who did it."

CHAPTER SIXTEEN

It was all anyone could talk about Monday morning. Some people refused to believe Stephanie and Erin were into each other and claimed that someone who wanted to embarrass Erin must have posted the picture. Other people wondered if Drew had been Erin's beard all along.

Adults flowed in and out of Headmaster Clarkson's office. When I passed by on my way to pre-calc, I recognized the Wheelers from the photos in Erin's house. Mrs. Wheeler kept her sunglasses on and walked ahead of her husband, who stayed in the doorway to speak with Headmaster Clarkson. Mr. Clarkson held on to Mr. Wheeler's hand like he never wanted to let go, the way the crazy girlfriend held on to Chris's in *Get Out*. He seemed to be taking this meeting far more seriously than he'd taken the one he had with my mother and me. It made sense. The Wheelers always contributed generously to Granger fund-raisers.

Stephanie and Erin weren't at school. But Noah was.

I approached him in the hallway between classes and did my best to act like I didn't know he was a scumbag.

"Hey, Noah," I said, holding on tight to my backpack strap so I wouldn't grab him by the neck or punch him in the face.

"Beej. Hey," Noah said. He was smiling widely, in spite of dark circles under his eyes. "How's it going?"

"Fine, thanks. Yourself?"

"Keeping busy," Noah said. I'll bet. His usually gelled chestnut-brown hair was fuzzy and unkempt.

"Keeping busy ruining people's lives, the snake!"

"Now, Reggie, we've got to see if Majidi can keep a cool head. He's got to be careful here and make sure Olson doesn't suspect anything."

"Have you talked to Stephanie?" I asked him, though I already knew he hadn't. Stephanie and I had been in touch all weekend, collecting information to back up my hunch that Noah was the cyberbigot.

"Yeah," he lied. "She's pretty upset. It's a shame about what happened." He wasn't smiling anymore, but he didn't look embarrassed or guilt-ridden either.

"Whoever did it is in for a world of trouble. They must think sending out those emails was really worth it," I said, working hard to keep my voice steady. I wanted to beat the crap out of him. He'd sent that email about me and outed his best friend, but he was acting like he'd done nothing wrong. He was acting like he hadn't made Stephanie cry, like he hadn't made Erin afraid to come to school, like he hadn't made my life miserable. He was acting like what he'd done to us, how we felt, didn't matter at all.

"I'm sure the IT department is looking into it," Noah said. He didn't smirk, but with a comment like that, he might as well have. "I hope Stephanie comes back for the board meeting tomorrow night. She's worked so hard on this project. I know it would mean a lot for her to present with Elle and me."

"I hope she does too." It made me queasy, pretending to be civil with a person so beneath human decency that he could crawl under a pregnant ant. "Sorry, I don't want to keep you from class."

Noah waved me off. "Physics is a breeze. It's okay if I'm a little late," he said. I felt sorry for the sucker who was his lab partner.

"If you talk to Stephanie again, let her know I say hi and I'm thinking of her." Stephanie had told me when he'd be in class, but Noah didn't need to know that.

"Of course. She'll appreciate your concern," he said before he strode down the hallway. I went in the opposite direction, toward the yearbook office, checking over my shoulder to make sure he wasn't following me.

* * *

Elle was leaning against the wall and reading something on her phone outside the yearbook office when I got there. Once I'd explained my theory about Noah to her, she was more than willing to help.

"Hey," she said. "We'll be quick. I know you're skipping Spanish right now."

"Whoa! You know my schedule?" I joked. She rolled her eyes but didn't answer my question as she took out her key card. She swiped it in the digital lock on the *Gazette/* yearbook office door. It beeped and unlocked. The lights automatically switched on when we entered.

The right side of the stuffy office was disorganized, with stacks of newspapers and boxes on a table. The left side was pristine and organized, no scattered papers or clutter to be seen. I followed Elle's lead to a computer on the corner on the clean side. Yearbook for the win!

I pulled up a chair next to Elle while she logged on. The desktop was full of tiny folders labeled by month.

"Erin said she thought the photo of her might be from the Halloween dance. That's what she recognized when it wasn't vomiting rainbows, anyway," Elle said as she clicked on a folder and scrolled down the list of images.

"How is she?" I asked, even though I knew exactly how she was feeling. Stephanie told me Erin hadn't picked up any of her calls or responded to any of her texts.

"She didn't say much. When she's hurt, she has a tendency to isolate herself," Elle said, clicking on image after image. "She's like Jessica in that way. We're going to go check on her tonight."

"That's good. Tell her I'm sorry, or . . . tell her I said this sucks, or . . . I don't know," I said, trying to find the right words. Erin and I weren't particularly close. Plus, no matter what happened between Erin and Stephanie, I was on Team Stephanie. If Erin tried to put Stephanie down for the sake of her own reputation, I wasn't going to bend over backward to make her feel comfortable. "Tell her there are people at school who have her back. And I'm one of them. But you know, less sappy than that."

"I think what you said will do fine," Elle said as she turned from the screen and grinned at me.

"Okay." I rubbed the back of my neck. Elle turned her attention back to the computer and hovered the mouse over files with the name Wheeler in them. "Did Erin tell you about Stephanie and her?"

"Not directly. I could tell there was someone else after Drew."

"How could you tell?"

"She seemed lighter? Less stressed during practice. Sometimes she was even downright giddy."

"*Giddy* is not exactly a word I'd associate with Erin," I admitted.

"I don't think she would either! It was nice. I know it's personal, but she and I have been through so much . . . I've told her about the guy I like. I wish she felt like she could have told me about whom she liked." Elle's eyes stayed focused on the list of JPEGs.

The guy she liked?

"Oh. Well, maybe she didn't want to admit her feelings to a friend yet, or even to herself," I said, watching her lips purse as she stared at the screen. "What advice did she have about the guy you like?"

"She said she thought it was sweet the way he blushes at the mention of my name. I think it's sweet too. A little corny, but sweet." As she clicked on a photo, she peeked at me from underneath her long eyelashes. "Kind of the way you're blushing now."

My face was burning up like Ghost Rider's fiery skull, but Elle kept a straight face as she turned back to study the photo in front of her. "I think this is it."

I glanced at the photograph of Erin and pulled out my phone to compare it to the GIF. The GIF was in black and white, but the photo was otherwise identical. "That's the one," I said, my face still hot. "Can you send it to me and Stephanie?"

"Yup. And I already forwarded you two the image my friend Alan took of Stephanie for the *Gazette*'s upcoming issue." Elle logged in to her Granger email and attached the file.

Behind us, the door beeped again. Elle and I both looked up to see Jessica.

"Hey," she said, her eyebrows rising in surprise.

"Hi, Jess," Elle said as she clicked send. I waved at Jessica to be polite.

"What are you guys doing in here?" Jessica inspected me momentarily before directing her attention to Elle. "Only members of the yearbook and newspaper staffs are allowed in the office."

"Elle is helping me figure out who sent those emails," I explained.

"Did you find anything?"

"We think so," Elle said. "Based on the info Erin and Stephanie gave us."

"You talked to Erin? How is she? Did she sound upset?" Jessica asked.

"You can ask her yourself," Elle replied. "I told her to expect us around six fifteen tonight, if that works for you?"

"Yeah, that works. I've got lots of evenings free now." So she and Will were definitely off again. "I feel so bad for her. Let me know if there's anything I can do," Jessica said.

"Thank you," I said. She felt so bad for *her*. She wouldn't have offered to help if an email about anyone else had been sent out.

Jessica licked her lips and nodded. But she didn't make eye contact with me.

"I think we have everything we need now," Elle said.

I hoped she was right.

CHAPTER SEVENTEEN

I was waiting for Sean in front of the auditorium. The board meeting had been moved there from the usual conference room because of the expected crowd. Sean's moms were already inside with mine, probably in the front row. Dozens of parents filed into the space. I recognized some of them from the meeting in my living room. A cynical part of me thought the crowd was larger now because a cyberbully had gone after two white girls this time, but I was a little relieved that I wouldn't be the sole focus of the meeting.

"Hey!" Sean smiled when he saw me standing there. "You made it."

"Last-minute decision."

"You going to say a few words?"

"No way." I had made that clear to my mom when I agreed to come. Public speaking freaked me out. Plus, I wouldn't know what to say.

"There's nothing good on TV, so we might as well watch this show," he said with a shrug. "I kind of want to see Mr. Clarkson sweat a little. I don't know if he's physically able to do so."

"Let's go find seats. Way in the back." I didn't know if Stephanie would show up. I had called her to make sure she got Elle's email, but she hadn't answered her phone or responded to my texts. Sean led me through the aisles to the back row, where we sat down. The stage had been set up for a town-hall-style meeting, with a long table and six chairs behind it for the board members. My mom and Sean's moms stood at the front of the center aisle near a microphone.

An angry buzz filled the room. Instead of the stuff we'd hear at games or school plays, where adults would talk about work, which kid was going to what college, where they could find the best SAT tutor or private tennis lessons, parents complained about how badly the school was handling the situation or how kids were out of control with technology.

Not many students were in attendance. Elle sat in the middle of the theater between her mom and dad. I thought about introducing myself but decided maybe now wasn't the greatest time.

Mr. and Mrs. Wheeler sat in the same row, but Erin wasn't with them. I wondered how she would handle things when she came back to school. She could just deny the rumors. Say the email was some sad joke concocted by a jealous person. She could say she was straight, and even if she wasn't, there was no way she would be with Stephanie Bergner. People would believe her—or at least pretend to. She could avoid Stephanie like the plague and go about her life as leader of the New Crew, a little tainted until she hosted a few more parties and all was forgotten.

Noah sat up front with his parents, who seemed oblivious to what a monster of a kid they had produced. Noah's father stood and spoke warmly with Sean's mom Hana.

"If you had laser vision, you'd have burned a hole in the back of Noah's neck by now," Sean said.

"Unfortunately I'm not Cyclops."

"Thank goodness. Scott Summers is such a crybaby."

"He's not so bad in *Astonishing X-Men*. Plus, spending nights with Emma Frost wouldn't be terrible. I'm more staring at Noah the way Charlie McGee would in *Firestarter*."

"Yeah, you kind of resemble a ten-year-old girl," Sean deadpanned. Headmaster Clarkson, Mr. Thompson, and four other members of the board sat in the chairs onstage. "Looks like the cockadoodie show is about to begin."

"Profanity bothers you?" I asked as the board members settled in.

"It has no nobility," Sean answered.

"Good evening," Mr. Clarkson said, leaning in to one of the microphones on the table. He waited until everyone had found a seat and quieted down. "Thank you for coming. I have heard from many of you these past two weeks, and we have a great deal to discuss. I apologize if I have not responded to all of your emails and voice mails, but I will do my best to follow up once we have more information regarding the, er . . . the images. I know you all have questions for me, but I would ask that you please wait until we have given you all the information we have before coming up to the microphone."

He explained that the school was organizing a full-day antibullying program to take place after spring break. He assured us that the IT department was working overtime to try to identify the IP address of the computer used in the anonymous emails.

"So you still don't know who did this?" Mom Jane yelled from the audience.

"Please, we can take questions after," Mr. Thompson said into his microphone.

"No. We don't yet know who did it," Headmaster Clarkson answered, in spite of Mr. Thompson's comment. The audience groaned.

"First we have a brief presentation from Ms. McCrea and a few students who have requested time to speak to us," Headmaster Clarkson announced. "After their presentation we will take a short recess and come back to listen to your questions and concerns. Ms. McCrea, the floor is yours."

Ms. McCrea got up from her seat in the front row and waited for Elle to join her at the microphone. Noah left his parents and went to the tech booth in the back. He gave me a small wave as he scurried past our row. I didn't wave back.

"Thank you. I'm so glad to see so many of you here tonight. I'd like to introduce Elle Powell, who will be speaking on behalf of the students who have signed a petition to change the current school mascot." Ms. McCrea moved away from the microphone and stood to the right of Elle.

"Thank you for your time," Elle said to the board members. She adjusted the microphone and held a piece of paper to read from. "I want to thank the parents for organizing this meeting and for encouraging me to say a few words about the school mascot. My friend Stephanie Bergner couldn't make it tonight." She paused to clear her throat. Everyone in that auditorium knew why Stephanie couldn't make it. "We were going to present together. I wouldn't be here speaking about this issue were it not for her tireless efforts.

"As Ms. McCrea said, my name is Elle Powell, and I am a junior. I have enjoyed my time at Granger. My teachers have been incredible, the facilities are extraordinary, I love playing for the varsity squash team, and I love being on the yearbook staff. That said, when I put on my uniform for squash matches, I represent Granger, but I don't feel our mascot necessarily represents the best of our community. Two hundred people signed our petition to change the Granger mascot. Many students and faculty agree that a change is welcome and that Granger—"

Mr. Thompson raised his hand to interrupt. "What is it that the students object to?"

Ms. McCrea touched Elle gently on the shoulder as she leaned into the microphone.

"William, with all due respect, if we could wait until Elle has finished, we will be able to answer your questions," she said. Mr. Thompson folded his arms across his chest. He had the exact same expression Will did when he didn't get his way. His brow furrowed and he leaned back in his chair like Will did on the bench when Coach wouldn't put him in.

Elle stood silent for a second. Ms. McCrea whispered something to her before backing away from the microphone. Just as Elle leaned in again, the door to the auditorium squeaked open and Stephanie Bergner let herself in. Elle lifted her head and smiled.

"Bergner makes it just in time for the double-team. What a move!"

"The dynamic duo of Powell and Bergner are ready to rumble!"

I turned to look at Noah, who stared at Stephanie in

disbelief. I wished I had eyes in the back of my head so I could watch him and Elle at the same time, but the main action was with Stephanie.

"I'm sorry I'm late," Stephanie said to the board as she walked over to Elle and Ms. McCrea.

"Fine, fine, let us carry on, please. What do those who signed the petition find so offensive?" Mr. Thompson asked again, checking his watch.

"The students who signed the petition object to the soldier's gun, sir," Elle said. "As well as to being known as the Gunners. We also object to the fact that people who do not currently attend the school seem to dominate the conversation regarding the mascot." She paused for a moment. "May we continue, Headmaster Clarkson?"

Mr. Clarkson nodded. Elle cleared her throat.

"What I love most about being a part of yearbook is that I have a chance to mold a part of Granger's history. The staff of *Our Time to Shine* gets to create a time capsule of school memories. I was curious to know whether the school had always had the Gunners as a mascot, so Stephanie and I researched Granger history in the library archives." Elle motioned for Noah in the booth to lower the lights and drop the projector screen. The board members turned to look at the screen.

"We are about to show you photographs from 1957, when Granger was still an all-boys school," Stephanie said. "Could we see the first slide, please?"

A black-and-white photograph was projected onto the screen. It showed Granger students, all of them white and male, standing on the bleachers at a football game. Four of the young men were shirtless, wearing war paint and headdresses straight out of Coachella.

"The Red Chief was the Granger mascot from the school's founding in 1897 until 1970." Elle gestured to the screen. "It is disappointing that the school I love waited until 1970 to change a mascot that is racist and dehumanizing to Native Americans and indigenous people. It is also a disappointing fact that many high school, college, and professional sports teams have such mascots to this day."

The next slide showed a blowup of the caption underneath the photograph. One name was highlighted in yellow: *Will Thompson, class of '57.* Mr. Thompson had his head turned to look up at the screen, so I couldn't see his face, but he didn't object to his photo being on display. There were, however, whispers among the audience.

"The mascot was changed in 1970 because of the efforts of the classes of '67, '68 and '69, who began a petition campaign in 1967, much like the one Stephanie Bergner began last year." Elle tilted her head in Stephanie's direction. "It is worth noting that Granger became co-ed in 1964 and was dealing with changes already. In reviewing the campaign from the sixties in the archived issues of the *Gazette*, we learned that some saw the mascot debate as frivolous or unimportant. But it was important enough to the student body, who spoke out to fight for it. If the school was able to change the mascot back then, why can't we do the same now? And this time, perhaps we can pick a symbol that speaks to who we are as a school and what we aspire to be: a safe, welcoming place where ideas and people are valued."

Elle motioned for Noah to turn off the projector. The lights came back on, and I blinked against the brightness. The board turned their chairs back around. I could see Mr. Thompson's smug face staring out at an unimpressed audience.

"Now, I realize that time marches on and people evolve," Elle said. "With that in mind, I do hope that the board will consider changing the mascot once again. Stephanie and I look forward to working with you and the student body to find a more appropriate symbol for our school. Thank you."

Sean and I stood up, along with many others in the audience, and applauded Elle as she went back to her seat. Ms. McCrea sat down too, but Stephanie stayed at the microphone.

"Ms. Bergner, did you have something to add?" Mr. Clarkson asked as the applause died down. This didn't seem like part of the official agenda, but there was no way Clarkson was going to deny Stephanie a chance to speak after the ordeal she'd been through.

"Yes, thank you," Stephanie said as she held up a manila folder. "I believe I know who composed the inappropriate images that were sent to the student body and would like to speak with you about it. Unless that person would like to reveal himself to you now?"

"Now, THIS is worth commenting for! What a show, Kevin! What. A. Show!"

The crowd gasped.

"I believe that is a conversation better held in private," Mr. Clarkson said. "Perhaps we should take a short break and reconvene in ten minutes. Ms. Bergner, if you could please meet me in my office."

"Of course," Stephanie said to Headmaster Clarkson. Then she turned to look straight at Noah. Some in the audience hadn't even sat back down yet. Now more people stood up to speak to each other, confusion and gossip swirling in the air as Stephanie left the auditorium.

"Way better than TV," Sean said. I twisted around in my seat to see Noah sneaking out of the tech booth and leaving the auditorium through the back. I stood up and shuffled by Sean.

"Where are you going?" he asked me.

"Bathroom," I lied. I wanted to see where Noah was slinking off to.

* * *

I walked down the dimly lit hallway toward Mr. Clarkson's office. Photographs of past Granger classes hung on the walls. It felt like the entirety of Granger history was watching me as I heard Noah confronting Stephanie around the corner.

"Why won't you talk to me?" Noah asked her as I stopped behind a column to listen. "Who do you think did it?"

"I'm going to wait until I speak to Headmaster Clarkson," Stephanie replied.

"You think it's me. You think I did it."

I didn't hear Stephanie say anything.

"I can't believe this. After everything I've done for you."

"Done for me?" Stephanie asked, incredulous.

"I have done everything I can to show you how much I care for you," Noah said, his voice cracking, making him sound like a little kid. "I joined you for every ridiculous cause you thought was worthy of your attention. I made sure the newspaper ran your opinion pieces even when the whole staff thought they were stupid and attention-seeking. I was the shoulder you cried on when you heard people calling you names."

"That doesn't mean I have to pursue a romantic relationship with you," Stephanie fumed. "I thought you were my friend. A friend wouldn't have done this, Noah!"

"A *friend* wouldn't have led me on," Noah said. He was almost shouting now. "That night when you asked me to take you to that stupid party, I was thrilled. I thought we were on a date. Finally, you were going to see me as more than your stupid canvassing buddy. What did you end up doing at the party? You left me. For that jock! I thought he was the guy you were always texting. Your stupid secret texts were for your stupid girlfriend, weren't they? What an idiot I was. I saw you and Erin in the library. When she pushed your hair back behind your ear and you blushed. You looked like a lovesick puppy."

"We thought we were alone," Stephanie said. "You took a simple gesture as an excuse to humiliate me. Do you have some delusional notion that you have a *right* to me?"

It was silent for a moment.

"What's in that folder?" he asked.

Stephanie didn't answer him.

"What's in it?" he asked.

"Get away from me!" Stephanie yelled.

"Hey!" I rushed around the corner. Noah was tugging on Stephanie's folder, but I pushed him away from her. He was breathing heavily, his face red.

"This doesn't concern you," Noah spat as I took my hands off his shoulders.

"It does. You sent that email about me," I said as he leaned against the wall. "Is this why? You were jealous that Stephanie hung out with me at a party?"

His usual forgettable, amiable smile was nowhere to be found. He looked at me with an empty stare that gave me a chill. "I didn't send that email about you."

"You're lying," I snarled.

"The photograph of me that you sent out was from the *Granger Gazette*," Stephanie said to Noah, holding up her folder, her voice quaking. "I was photographed recently for an article about the mascot, but the new issue of the newspaper isn't out yet. The photo of Erin that was sent out was taken for this year's yearbook. The yearbook staff does not have access to the *Gazette*'s materials and vice versa. There's only one student who has access to both. The layout editor of both of those publications."

Noah's eyes darted between Stephanie and me. He knew Stephanie always saw a project through to the end. There was no way she was going to half-ass an investigation.

"Ms. Bergner." I heard Mr. Clarkson's voice and turned my head to see him and Ms. McCrea walking toward us. "There was something you wanted to share. In private," he said, nodding at Noah and me.

"Yes, sir," she said.

Mr. Clarkson brushed past Noah to unlock his office door. Ms. McCrea gently put her arm around Stephanie's shoulders, and they both disappeared into the office. Headmaster Clarkson shut the door behind them.

Noah paced back and forth, gritting his teeth.

"You piece of—" I stopped myself from cursing him out in front of the headmaster's office. "You didn't think anyone would find out?"

"Shut up," he whispered to me.

"Me shut up? Oh, dude, I am going to make you wish you never sent that garbage about me and—"

Noah stopped in his tracks. "I didn't send that email about you. Trust me, I liked it, and kudos to the guy who made it . . . but I didn't have anything to do with that."

CHAPTER EIGHTEEN

The news of Noah's expulsion was the latest in a string of juicy gossip items that had gripped the Granger campus, but no one was particularly upset. He didn't have many friends, other than Stephanie. I could tell she was sad when I'd ask her how she was doing, but she put on this brave face at school and pretended Noah had never existed. She was keeping herself busy, flitting from class to club. She always seemed to be around people. I didn't know why. I'd spent the last weeks wanting to retreat and be alone.

"Bijan, can you stay behind for a moment?" Ms. McCrea asked as Friday's history class came to a close.

"I have to pack up and catch the bus with the team," I said, jerking my thumb to the door as my classmates rushed out. We were driving to New Hampshire for the

New England tournament that afternoon to stay overnight at a Holiday Inn near the tourney.

"This will only take a moment," she said, standing up behind her desk.

"So like an hour," Sean whispered to me before he left. "I'll see you at the game."

Ms. McCrea met me in the middle of the room.

"I'm sorry about my paper being late," I said. It was a week overdue, and I wasn't going to get to it over the weekend.

"While I have been waiting on your assignment, that's not what I want to talk to you about," Ms. McCrea said. "I want to ask you how you're doing."

"Fine," I said, looking briefly away from her and taking interest in a United Nations poster. If she needed to worry about anyone, it was Erin Wheeler, who hadn't been at school for a week. Her absence was fueling rumors. Sean said he heard some knucklehead in the ceramics studio claim that Erin was being sent to a Catholic boarding school somewhere in California.

"You've been quiet in class," Ms. McCrea continued. I didn't realize I was ordinarily a chatterbox. "Your work hasn't been up to your usual standards. I wondered if maybe you want to talk about anything."

"Well, they caught Noah, so there's nothing to talk about," I said.

There was something that still bothered me about what Noah had said before Headmaster Clarkson asked him into his office: Why would he deny sending the email about me and admit to sending the other one? What if he really didn't do it?

"Yes, while I'm relieved Mr. Olson was asked to leave, I want you to know that there are resources and people here for you. Ms. Jacobs, for instance—"

"I'll keep that in mind," I said, holding my hands up. I didn't need to talk to the guidance counselor, even though she was really nice and pronounced my name correctly. There was nothing to talk about. If anything, Noah should have talked to her before he decided to go on a psycho GIF-creating spree.

"Okay," Ms. McCrea said, letting the issue drop. "I take it the tournament will be keeping you pretty busy this weekend and you may not have your paper ready by Monday?"

"Would Wednesday work?" I was doing my best to catch up in my other classes, but some days the workload felt insurmountable.

"Wednesday will be fine. But later than that and we'll have to have a discussion about what we can do to get you up to speed."

"Thank you, and yes, I totally understand," I said, relieved.

"Good luck! We're all rooting for you. On and off the court." She held a hand in the air for me to high-five. I slapped it, even though it felt kind of corny. I believed her when she said she was rooting for me.

"Hey, all-star," Elle called from down the nearly deserted hallway. There were only a few straggler freshmen waiting around to be picked up.

"You're the all-star," I said, shoving *The Scarlet Letter* into my backpack before shutting my locker. "Speaking truth to power like a boss. I'm glad I bumped into you." I pulled two trades from my backpack and handed them to her. We'd been exchanging comics in English class since Erin's party.

"I loved *This One Summer*, so thank you for that," I said. "This one is my pick for you."

"Paper Girls! Nice one," she said.

"You've read it already, haven't you?" I asked.

"How did you know?"

"Your eyes didn't light up like when I gave you *Embroideries* and *Astro City: The Tarnished Angel*," I said.

"Okay, yes, I am all caught up with Paper Girls. I am, however, happy to revisit it," she said, taking the book from me. "Are you excited for the tournament?"

"I'm nervous."

"You? Nervous? Never," she said with a grin.

"BANG! Powell with the smooth line. Majidi may be coming undone right before our eyes!"

"He is going to have to bring his A game here, Kevin. He is going to have to—"

Shut up, guys. Much respect, but shut up. I've got this.

Elle handed me an envelope with my name on it.

"What's this?"

"I took it upon myself to be your not-so-secret psych."

I opened the envelope and laughed. A smiling Chuck E. Cheese mouse stared at me from a printed coupon, offering me a two-dollar discount on any large pizza and a hundred tokens for twenty-five dollars.

"I kind of want to frame this," I said.

"I figured you might need them when you get back," she said softly. "*We* might need them."

"Thank you. I hope your Skee-Ball game is up to snuff." I opened my arms and she leaned into me for an embrace. We held each other. Not too long, but long enough to feel that this was the start of something. Something big, I hoped.

"To be clear, the coupons are symbolic—you don't actually want me to take you to Chuck E. Cheese's on our first date?" I asked as we let go of each other.

"No. That place is for babies."

"Phew! Okay, just needed to be sure."

* * *

"Best Celtic of all time?" Todd asked from the seat behind Marcus and me on the bus. "For me, and I know this is going to be a controversial pick . . . Brian Scalabrine."

"Get out of here," Marcus said with a laugh. We had been on the road for a little over an hour, and so far so good. Drew sat up front by Coach to avoid being tormented by Will about Erin dumping him for Stephanie.

"You know that's not a real answer. But Scal is a great commentator," Todd said. "I guess I have to go with Larry Bird." That, at least, made sense.

"Bird is a legend," I conceded. "He and Magic saved the NBA. He could shoot from everywhere. A great trash talker too. But the best Celtic of all time has to be Bill Russell."

"Over Bird?" Todd asked.

"Yeah!" I said. "Bill Russell invented blocking! He helped the Cs win eleven championships and was MVP five times!"

"Yeah, but Russell was playing in the sixties," Todd said. "I mean, there wasn't that much competition."

"What is that supposed to mean?" Marcus asked. "Because there were fewer black players back then?"

"Well, yeah. That and shorter shorts," Todd said, doing his best to backpedal.

"Their shorts were just as tiny in the eighties," I argued. "But even if Russell had played in the eighties, he would have dominated."

"I have to go with the Truth," Marcus said. "He gave his all every night when he played."

"Only one championship ring for Pierce, though," Todd said.

"Hey, in the age of LeBron, one ring means something," Marcus countered. "How do you know how short those shorts were, Beej?"

"The change in regulation length of basketball shorts can be attributed to the Fab Five. Juwan Howard, Jalen Rose, Jimmy King, Ray Jackson, and Chris Webber all wore long shorts at Michigan, and it caught on."

"Why do you know that?" Todd asked.

"He's a real student of the sport," Marcus said.

"I try."

"Okay, then," Marcus said, trying to stump me. "Name two WNBA teams." A lesser fan would have faltered.

"The Minnesota Lynx have been dominating the past few seasons, mostly because of Maya Moore's leadership. Since the departure of the Seattle SuperSonics, the Seattle Storm have been *the* professional basketball team in the city. And I've missed seeing Tamika Catchings on the court since she retired."

"Wow!" Todd said. He grinned and shook his head. "Wow, wow, wow."

Marcus slapped me on the back and laughed. "You're a basketball nerd!" he said.

"Correction: basketball *savant*," I protested.

"Nerd," Marcus replied. "But it's cool."

The bus slowed down to exit the highway. The bright lights of the Holiday Inn parking lot cut through the darkness.

Coach stood to address us from the front of the bus.

"All right, we're going to check in, drop off our stuff, grab some dinner, and then go straight to bed. No funny business tonight. Got it?" He pointed to the back. I turned my head to see that Will had his hand raised.

"Yeah, Thompson. What?"

"What exactly do you mean by funny business, Coach?" Will asked, smirking.

"I mean I have no time for clowns. I see or hear about any of you drinking, doping, sneaking out to see a girl-friend, your ass is benched. We understand each other?"

Will didn't have a comment for that.

"I have picked your roommates for you, so don't worry your pretty little heads about making arrangements with your buddies."

"Maybe we'll get to room together," I said to Marcus.

"Doubtful," Marcus whispered. "The two of us walking around alone at night in New Hampshire . . . we might have problems."

"Oh," I muttered. I hadn't spent much time in New Hampshire, but it didn't strike me as a place that was ready to welcome me with open arms. I could be wrong, but that Live Free or Die motto has always struck me as too intense.

"B," Coach said, and my head snapped up.

"Present!"

"You're rooming with Young."

CHAPTER NINETEEN

The hotel room was basic: two double beds separated by a wooden nightstand with a gray lamp on it, across from a chest of drawers that doubled as a stand for the TV and coffeemaker. A small desk and office chair by the window and stain-free beige carpet really brought the room together. While the decor was nothing to write home about, it was cool to be on the road for a game. I'm sure the Celtics stayed at the Ritz, but it made me feel like a big deal to have my room paid for.

Drew silently claimed the bed by the window by throwing his bag on top of it. As I dropped my duffel on the other bed and started to unpack, Drew grabbed the remote and flopped down to channel surf.

"Do you mind if I take the top drawer?" I asked.

He grunted.

"Sorry, is that a yes or a no?"

"Yeah, whatever. I don't care." He flipped through the stations so fast, I doubted he could actually see what was on.

I hadn't packed much, but I placed my folded clothes in the small bureau drawer.

Drew finally settled on a horror movie.

"*Zombie Killers Part Three*. A modern classic," I said, sitting on the edge of my bed to watch. "Wasn't the fifth one awful? McNair, *the* zombie hunter, comes back from the dead and becomes the very thing he's hated for years. It had so much potential. I don't get how they made such a boring movie out of that premise."

"I haven't seen any of them," Drew said out of the corner of his mouth. Minimal effort, but it was better than grunting.

"Not one? That's crazy!"

"I don't have a lot of time for movies," Drew said, still staring at the TV.

We watched McNair's ex-wife rise from the grave to try to eat him. I mouthed the dialogue along with McNair: "*'You always were a man-eater.'*" He then proceeded to fight off the surrounding zombies with his spear as Hall & Oates's "Maneater" played in the background.

"Just like a woman to chew a man up and spit him out," I said in unison with McNair, when he almost got bitten.

"I hear that," Drew muttered.

"Yeah. Women. You can't live with them, you can't live with undead versions of them." I held up my hand for a high five. Drew ignored me. I put my hand down and looked at the painting of a sailboat on the wall, wondering if anyone on that boat had to share quarters with someone they didn't have much in common with. Maybe the painting would start coming to life like in *1408* and Drew and I could team up to face the haunted room.

The hotel phone rang. I answered, grateful for the distraction.

"That was Coach," I told Drew after I'd hung up. "We're supposed to meet in the lobby in ten minutes for team dinner."

"I'm not hungry."

"Coach said we have to be there."

"Coach says I have to do a lot of things, but sometimes I'd like a break."

"Is it because of the whole Erin thing?"

He turned to glare at me.

"You don't feel like being around the guys?"

We stared at each other until he mean-mugged me like John Wall glaring at a ref after a lousy call.

"Got it," I said. "No bringing up She Who Must Not Be Named."

I looked away from him and focused on the TV. McNair was sobbing over his decapitated ex-wife, her torso in his arms, her limbs strewn in front of him.

"There are five of these movies?"

"Yep! The sixth one comes out this summer. Sean and I already preordered tickets."

"I bet you two did," he said, but I noticed he didn't change the channel.

* * *

Coach brought us to a no-frills pizza spot near the hotel and ordered seven large pies for the team. It seemed like a lot at first, but Todd put five slices away in as many minutes.

"Slow down, Todd," Coach said. "We can always order more."

"Or you can have some of Drew's," Will suggested from the other end of the table. A few bites were missing from Drew's one slice, which lay limply on its grease-soaked paper plate.

"You must be sick of pizza, right, Drew?" Will went on, a gleam in his eye. "You eat it with the other busboys?"

Drew's face reddened. He picked up his slice and took a giant bite of it, staring Will down as he chewed.

Coach didn't defend Drew. No one did. What was wrong with having a job? Will Thompson got to act like a jerk because his family paid for the privilege? I'd had enough of Will, even if his comments were directed at my not-so-favorite roommate.

"Your face probably made him lose his appetite," I said to Will. "It's made me lose mine."

"Young Majidi with a swift comeback, even if it is a little juvenile."

"Kids today. They just don't understand the finesse of trash talking, Kevin."

Will leaned forward in his seat. I thought he was about to jump across the table to get to me, but he let his words do the job. "You're still here? Homeland Security hasn't picked you up yet?"

Coach slammed his fist on the table. "That's enough!" he yelled. The guys working behind the pizza counter stopped what they were doing to stare at us. For a few moments the only sound in the whole place came from Fox News on TV. Coach Johnson wasn't done. "You're on the same team! Act like it!"

"Sorry, Coach," Will said. He didn't even look my way.

"Can we get through this weekend without you all tearing each other down? You think we can save some of that for the other teams?" Coach asked, his voice at a more tempered volume. The guys gave stiff nods as he looked around the table, pausing extra long on Drew, Will, and me. When he was done, he gave the waiter a small wave to let him know everything was fine.

"Now I'd like to talk to you about tomorrow's game, if you don't mind?" Coach asked.

"Sure, Coach," Marcus said, his voice oozing disappointment. "The game. That's what's important."

"That's right, Marcus," Coach said, not picking up on

the sarcasm. I felt like a preschooler on a time-out. It wasn't right that no one was sticking up for Drew. "We're playing Mercer Day tomorrow," Coach went on. "Last time, we beat them by a hair, but they play dirty. We know it, they know it, but the refs up here don't."

I didn't know much about Mercer Day aside from their reputation as a last-resort private school for rich kids with not-so-hot grades or who had been kicked out of other prep schools. Mercer Day had a good sports program, especially because it was padded with nineteen-year-old seniors who needed to repeat a year.

"If we're going to beat them, we're going to have to be smart, and we're going to have to talk to each other on the court," Coach said. "You have to communicate with each other on defense." He went over some other strategy points. The whole time, Will sat there smirking at me. He looked like he had his own plans for Mercer Day.

* * *

We got back to the hotel around ten. Will walked ahead of the rest of us, including Coach, to greet some friends in the lobby.

"That's Eric Pennington and Mike Danton from Mercer Day," Marcus said to me as Will laughed and slapped hands with two beefy dudes who looked like they were both training to audition for WWE.

"They're in high school?" I asked. Even Todd, who was taller than both of them, looked a little intimidated.

"Eric, the bulky kid with the red baseball cap and lazy eye, still plays for Mercer. Mike, the taller one with the stupid pop-star haircut, finally graduated last year. He goes to college around here." From the scowl on Marcus's face, I could tell he hadn't enjoyed playing against them in the past.

"Looks like the away team really puts an emphasis on bulking up."

"Sure. Like the way the East German Olympic teams used to 'bulk up,' Kevin."

Coach noticed Will chatting it up with our archrivals.

"Thompson! Get over here," he shouted, waving Will back to join the rest of the team. Will obliged, but not before he told Eric and Mike, loudly, that he'd see them later that night.

Eric sneered at me, and then he and Mike left the hotel. Either word of my incredible skills had gotten around the private school league, or Will had let them know that I was on his list and should be on theirs too.

"Okay, it's time to hit the hay," Coach said. "Go to your rooms, get a good night's sleep, and be dressed and ready in the lobby at nine a.m. I trust I don't have to babysit you fellas all night. Remember, school rules apply here. We may be off campus, but that doesn't mean you get to act like there aren't consequences for your actions. We understand each other?"

"Yes, Coach," we mumbled. Will didn't say anything, but he turned his head to see if his friends were still waiting for him.

"Okay, then. Let's go." Coach led the way to the elevators.

* * *

After a low-key night eating leftover pizza and watching *The Late Show* with Marcus and Todd on the sixth floor, I said good night and headed for my room at about one thirty. I took the stairs back to the fourth floor. Just as I walked through the fire doors into the hallway, the elevator bell dinged and a glassy-eyed Will and his Mercer Day buddy Eric came spilling out. I had to pass them in the hallway to get to my room, and I was considering heading back to the stairs and sleeping with Todd and Marcus.

"Hey! Look who id izzz!" Will shouted, slurring his words.

"Hey," I said as they approached me. "I'm heading to bed."

"But isso early," Will said. "Why don' you come hang with us?"

"Yeah, me and my guys are down the hall," Eric said. "We're going to relax, throw a few back, blow off some steam." He wasn't as drunk as Will, but he couldn't be bothered to fake a smile around me.

"Sounds like a good time, but I better get some sleep," I said. Did they think I was stupid enough to go hang out alone in a room with them? "Big game tomorrow and everything." I tried to squeeze past them. Eric blocked my path.

"Why don't you want to party with us?" he asked. "You think you're better than us or something?"

Will snickered behind him.

"I'm tired. That's all." They inched closer.

"Is that right?" Eric asked, looking over his shoulder. "He says he's tired."

"Well, *I'm* tired of his people coming over here and ruining the country, Eric." Will suddenly sounded a lot more sober. His smile turned into a sneer. "How about you?"

"Yeah, I am too," Eric said before he turned back to me. He smelled like tobacco and whiskey, and his breath was warm against my face. "Real tired. Why don't you go back to Mexico and take a siesta?"

"Wrong people, Eric," Will said. "The other kind of brown. The banned ones."

"Even better! Hell, we'd probably get a Medal of Honor if we rough him up. Who'd miss him?"

I tried to back away. If I made a run for it, could I get down the stairs without them catching up to me? Where was my key card? I wouldn't have time to unlock the door if I didn't know where my key card was. I could fight them, but Eric was a beefy dude. I wouldn't last long.

Eric grabbed hold of my shoulder and pushed me backward with his forearm against my chest. I tried to get away, and I wanted to yell, but the fear wouldn't let me. My limbs were frozen and my thoughts were on repeat: *What are they going to do to me? Oh God, what are they going to do to me?*

I heard a door click open.

Drew stood in the doorway of our room, looking out at us. "We get it, you guys are real tough. Now can you keep it down so we can all get some sleep?"

Eric took his forearm off my chest but kept hold of a shoulder, digging his fingers deep into the muscle while slapping my other shoulder like we were pals. I tried to jerk away, but he was too strong.

"We were going to show Beej a good time," Will said. "Want to join us?"

Drew's right eye twitched, but he played it cool.

"You heard what Coach said. School rules apply here. Besides, we need him for tomorrow's game." It was really comforting to watch two white guys debate why I should or shouldn't get beat up based entirely on what I could do for them. "You remember what team you play for, Will?"

"The same team they let your white-trash ass play for," Will said with a chuckle. "The real question is, what team does Erin play for?"

Drew's bored expression didn't change. Will shook his head. "Let Aladdin go," he ordered Eric.

Eric's grip on me loosened. I tore away and made a bee-line for the room while Eric and Will laughed.

As soon as I was inside, Drew closed the door casually, as if there were nothing to be worried about. Once it was closed, though, he sprang into action, fastening the chain. He looked through the peephole to see if they had gone. "Bring me something to keep the door shut," he said as he leaned against it.

I carried over the desk chair.

"That's not going to keep anyone out!" he yelled.

"Help me move the desk, then!"

He grunted as we carried the small desk over to block the door.

"You need me for the game tomorrow, huh?" I said as I paced across the small room, adrenaline rushing through me. "That's the only reason I shouldn't get beaten to a pulp, or worse?"

"Look," Drew said. "The two of us could take Will, but we couldn't take Steroid McGillicuddy and however many of his friends decided to come out and join the fun." He took a deep breath. "This wouldn't happen if you didn't mouth off so much."

"Oh, really?" I yelled. "I should let people do whatever they want to me and just take it?"

Drew walked closer. The two of us stood in the center of the room, staring each other down.

"You think I don't want to tell Will Thompson to shove

his shit back up his ass every once in a while? You think Marcus doesn't want to put his fist through Will's perfect teeth on occasion?"

"You and Will were pretty chummy when you and I got into it. That's around the time everyone had a photo of me looking like a terrorist. Did he send out that email, and did you know all about it?"

"If Will sent that email, he didn't tell me," Drew said, his face reddening. "Someone probably sent it because you annoyed them with your self-righteous petition. Elle and Stephanie can be involved in that kind of stuff because they've got the money to say what they like. You and I can't afford to. Don't you get that?"

I just stared at him.

"I don't like being accused of doing things I haven't done," he continued. "You know I was called to Headmaster Clarkson's office four times because of that stupid email? My mom even asked me if I sent it. My mom, who already has to deal with so much crap at her job to support us, now has to worry that I'm going to get kicked out of Granger." Drew slammed his fist on the desk. I was surprised the wood didn't splinter. "You're messing up my life. You get that? I'm at that school to put the stupid orange ball in the hoop and that's it. I haven't heard a thank you yet for saving your butt just now either."

Drew and I glared at each other, but it no longer felt uncomfortable. We were going to be real.

"It's hard to thank you when I know you'd let Will and his Mercer buddies beat me up if I wasn't going to help you win tomorrow."

"I wouldn't. I have a conscience. Besides, if anything happened to you, I'd probably get blamed for it."

"Yeah," I shot back, my voice dripping with disdain. "I can't imagine what it's like to be blamed for something people who look like you did."

"That's not the same. I know what you're getting at. I don't care if you're Muslim." He sat on his bed but looked at me. "You know what those guys out there think? They think people like you aren't apologetic enough. With everything on the news, they're not buying that 'peaceful religion' rhetoric. They don't feel like they have to be politically correct when the facts are staring them in the face."

"They think that way or you think that way?" I said, standing in front of him with my fists clenched. He didn't answer. "I tell you what, Drew. I'll apologize when you apologize for every guy who looks like you who shoots up a movie theater, a church, or a school or drives a car into a crowd of peaceful protestors. How's that for a fair deal?"

We stood staring at one another, breathing heavily and waiting for the other to make a move.

"Look, it's late. We've got to play tomorrow," Drew finally said. "Can we save this argument for the bus ride home?"

I went into the bathroom and slammed the door behind me. Noise from the TV filled the room. I brushed my teeth so hard, my gums bled.

I left the bathroom and crossed to my side of the room by the glow of ESPN. I crawled under the covers and lay there in silence. Drew didn't make a move to turn off the NBA highlights show he was watching, but I was too wired to sleep anyway.

"It's just you and your mom?" I asked.

"I thought our 'getting to know you' time was done for today," Drew said, his eyes fixed on the TV. "But yeah. It's the two of us. Why?"

"It's just my mom and me too."

"Maybe we've got the same deadbeat dad?" Drew joked. "Mine's a real piece of work. A guy named Tim who would rather play keno and drink than hang out with his kid. What's the deal with yours?"

"My dad passed away," I said, turning away from him to try to sleep.

"Oh. I, uh . . . Sorry." He did sound sorry.

"It happened a long time ago," I said. "Sorry about your dad too."

"Yeah, so am I." We didn't say anything for a while, but the TV stayed on, the Buffalo Wild Wings commercials beginning to lull me to sleep.

"Thanks for not telling the guys about my fight with Erin at her party," Drew said.

He'd kept that thank you under his hat for a while, but I'd take it.

"You're welcome."

"So you're friends with Bergner?" Drew asked.

"Yeah," I said without hesitation.

"Did she ever talk to you about, uh . . . you know, her and Erin?"

"No. She didn't."

"You repeat any of this and I tell everyone you pissed your bed, got it?"

"Got it." I rolled my eyes. The last thing I needed to worry about was the student body thinking I was a bed wetter when they had formed such kind opinions of me already.

"I kind of thought there was something going on between Erin and Bergner for a while. I asked her about in the beginning of the year and she said I was being ridiculous. But I wasn't, was I?

"I called her a few days ago. I should have been the one allowed to be upset, but she started crying and I felt sorry for her. Isn't that messed up? She's got a thing for someone else, and I feel sorry for her. I mean, I may have a never-there dad, but her folks aren't that far from being in Tim's club of negligent parents.

"I asked her if she needed anything, and she started crying again. She went on and on about how she'd never cheated on me, like they'd never gotten physical or whatever until she broke it off with me . . . but it's so embarrassing." Drew paused for a second before continuing. "Not that she's into chicks. I mean, whatever. It's high school, people got to figure their stuff out. I didn't plan on us getting married. If she's gay or bi, so be it . . . but she picked Busted Bergner over me? How does that even make sense? Isn't Bergner like captain of the chess team?"

"Something like that," I said, grinning a little in the dark. Drew couldn't believe he had lost Erin to a chess nerd. "But isn't it better that you have your senior year free to date whoever you want? So long as the crap that comes out of your mouth doesn't get in the way."

"I guess. It was nice to have a taste of the good life, though. Pool parties, trips to her house on the Cape . . . Plus, she wasn't a snob, you know? She's not like Jessica, who acts like she's superior to everyone."

"Yeah, I've gotten that vibe from her," I agreed. "Why do Erin and Elle hang out with her?"

"No idea. She's so fake around them, but she's a totally miserable person. I mean, you'd have to be to hook up with Will on the regular."

"Gross," I said.

"Match made in heaven until he broke it off. Anyway, Erin calmed down after we talked. I kind of realized we don't have a whole lot in common. I think we kind of used each other. I liked her lifestyle, and she liked having the safety of being in a straight relationship. After that Noah kid sent out that email, I could understand that better. You must be relieved they caught him."

Relieved. Sure. Tonight had definitely proved I had nothing to worry about anymore.

"He said he didn't send the picture of me," I replied.

"And you believe that freak?"

Deep down, I did.

CHAPTER TWENTY

"Breakfast buffet! Wish I had more of an appetite," I said as Drew and I ambled into the Holiday Inn dining area dressed in our Granger warm-up suits. I took a plate and looked at the wide array of pastries, fruit, and yogurt cups. It was a sliver of joy in an otherwise lousy trip, but I didn't think I'd be able to get much down after the night I'd had.

"We're not supposed to load up on sugar," Drew said. "Coach says we'll be more likely to crash later." I took the tongs and placed a mini Danish on my plate. I held another above Drew's plate, waiting for him to object. "Okay, maybe one won't hurt."

I dropped the pastry on his plate and kept the line moving. Most of the team was already sitting at a table with Coach. He was wearing a suit and tie, his thinning hair combed back Pat Riley fashion.

"You going to tell Coach about what happened last night?" Drew asked as I piled hash browns on my plate.

"I had planned on it, yeah." I expected him to object or tell me to sit on it until we got home. Maybe he thought I was a snitch, but I wasn't going to let Will push me around anymore.

"I'll back you up," he said.

I was stunned. "Thanks."

"That guy's got it coming. Hanging out with the enemy and all."

"Right. Your show of concern is duly noted."

"You know what I mean." Drew picked up a plain yogurt cup. "Do you see him?"

I finished loading up my plate with some fruit and looked around the dining area. No sign of Will.

"Maybe he got arrested," I said as Drew and I walked over to the team's table. I sat beside Todd. He had a black piece of duct tape covering the Gunners mascot on his warm-up jacket.

"Morning," Marcus said as Drew sat next to him. Marcus had also duct-taped over the mascot on his jacket. "Did you get any sleep?"

I hadn't slept much. When I'd looked in the mirror that morning, I'd seen dark circles under my bloodshot eyes.

"A little." I didn't want to tell him in front of everyone what Will and his goon had done, and definitely not before the game. I wanted to talk to Coach in private, but he was writing in his playbook, probably making last-minute changes to our game plan while he ate his eggs.

"Don't be nervous. Play your game and you'll do great," Marcus said.

"It's our last chance to win for Granger, and we're cool as cukes," Todd said. If anything, I wanted to win for him and Marcus. These were their last games in Granger uniforms, and even though they didn't like the mascot that represented them, they had represented the school and team with dignity and honor.

"Do you have any duct tape?" I asked Marcus.

"It's in my sports bag," he said with a wry smile. "I'll get it to you in the locker room."

Drew pretended not to hear us, focusing on stuffing his face full of protein. He hadn't touched the Danish yet. I guessed he was saving the best for last.

"Young is waffling on more than whether or not he wants to eat his Danish, Reggie. Waffling. See what I did there?"

"Kevin."

"Because it's breakfast time?"

"We've talked about this. If you have to explain a joke . . ."

"I know, I know, then it's not funny. I'm doing my best with what we're working with here. Let me know when it's game time."

I was pouring ketchup on my hash browns when Will walked in like one of the zombies McNair hunted. He was wearing Ray-Ban sunglasses and his HERE TO STAY T-shirt.

His Granger warm-up pants were unsnapped on the sides. He ignored all the food on the buffet table and headed straight to the coffeepot.

"Morning, Will!" Drew shouted. Will recoiled, almost spilling the coffee. He took a seat as far away from Coach as he could get. "You get a good night's rest?"

Will didn't answer him. He took a sip from his cup and rubbed his temple.

"Will," Coach said, still looking at his playbook. "You hungover, son?"

"No, Coach," Will said, his voice hoarse.

"I can't hear you. What's that?"

"I said no, Coach."

Coach looked Will up and down in disgust.

"I suppose you're just tired?"

"Yeah. The mattresses here do nothing for me."

"That's fine. You can get plenty of rest on the bench," Coach said, taking a sip of orange juice.

"What? Coach, I'm fine! Really, I—"

"This is it, Thompson. We've had a good ride together, but the team can't make any more excuses for you. I can't make any more excuses for you." Coach pointed his finger at Will. "You want to make a mess out of your own life, by all means go ahead. You've got a hell of a start. But there's no way you're taking this moment away from these young men or from me. B, you're starting in Will's place."

I was starting! I nodded but didn't make a sound. None of the guys at the table did. I did my best to keep the grin off my face.

"Coach, come on. I can play," Will croaked.

"I'll think about it when B needs a break, but I'd rather put in someone who cares about this team and not about getting his jollies on road trips," Coach said. Then he turned back to his playbook. The discussion was over and Will knew it. He rested his head on the table.

* * *

When we walked out onto the university's court, we were met by a packed house of students, faculty, parents, and friends clapping and screaming at higher decibels than I'd ever heard before.

I looked for my mom, Sean, and his parents in the stands. They sat in one of the middle rows near our bench. I waved. Mom waved her Granger pom-pom at me. Sean held up a sign that read *Eye of the Tiger, Beej!* which cracked me up.

We got into our layup lines and began to warm up. Will stood behind me. "I had fun last night," he said over my shoulder.

I ignored him and waited my turn.

"Some of my buddies were sorry they couldn't meet

you. See if you can spot them today. It's great that you'll have plenty of time on the court with them."

I caught my pass and ran up to take my shot. The ball bounced off the rim. I almost never missed my layups. I had to get out of my own head. I had to get *Will* out of my head, or I would be off for the whole game. I watched the Mercer Day team do the same drill. Eric dribbled to his basket and made his shot with no trouble at all.

When the whistle blew and the game started, Will's buddies lost no time. Eric was guarding me, and he looked like he would eat me alive if I let him get too close. He was itching for the fight he hadn't gotten the night before. He didn't let me breathe.

"Mercer Day's number two is a tenacious defender! It is going to be hard to get the ball to Majidi under that kind of pressure."

Marcus found Todd posted up under the basket for a few easy buckets in the first quarter, but Mercer Day tightened their defense and made it hard for Marcus to keep feeding Todd in the paint. They had good perimeter shooters, and what they lacked in rebounding, they made up for in fouls and trash talk.

"I heard you got the nuke codes on you," Eric said to me as Todd took his foul shots.

By the beginning of the third quarter, the score was tied at 34. Marcus had a monster of a game, leaving it all on the floor. He was making sure he was going out a legend.

I managed to score twice, make five assists, and grab three rebounds.

When I tried to push off Eric to run a play, he grabbed my arm to stay with me.

"Come on, ref! Open your eyes!" Coach shouted, his face red as he paced the sideline. "This kid is grabbing all over my player!"

"Don't let them push you around!" I heard my mom yell when the ref handed me the ball. I inbounded to Marcus and darted down the court before Eric could reach me. He couldn't keep up this intensity all game. If I kept running him around, I would eventually wear him down.

Marcus was stuck at the top of the key, but I still couldn't shake Eric. Todd came out to set a pick for me. I cut through the lane, caught the ball, and drove in for a layup. I wasn't missing this one. But as I went up, a bulldozer slammed into me. I fell to the court, banging my hip hard. Eric landed on top of me.

"Try and make a layup on me again. Then we'll see what happens," he spat, bouncing to his feet.

"Two shots!" the ref shouted. He blew his whistle. I got up and gingerly approached the free-throw line. The crowd behind the basket began to chant. At first I didn't register what they were saying. Then it grew louder.

"U.S.A.! U.S.A.! U.S.A.!"

The chants were mostly coming from one row. Will's buddy Mike stood with some guys who looked too old to be high school students. They had wrapped athletic towels on their heads and wore fake beards. One of them held up a poster-sized version of the terrorist photo of me. I looked over at the bench. Will laughed unapologetically, freely, with absolute glee.

The ref passed me the ball. I wanted to hurl it at Will. I wanted to scream. I wanted to run into the stands and rip up the poster. Instead, I dribbled twice, focused on the basket, and shot the ball. It went in and my "fans" were silenced.

"I'm going to call a time-out after you make this shot," Marcus said to me from behind. "They're assholes. But you don't cry out here!" he commanded. "You don't let them see you cry out here." I hadn't realized my eyes were welling up. I nodded as the ref passed me the ball for my second shot. Will's friends began to chant again, and more of them held posters. I shot the ball and missed. The crowd cheered wildly. Eric boxed me out by pushing me down with his arms, another flagrant foul.

"Majidi is down! He is down!"

"You never want to see this kind of thing in our beloved sport, Kevin."

The ref blew the whistle again, calling a technical foul.

"Who has paid off this ref? That was a flagrant foul! Unbelievable!"

"Is there nothing sacred in the game of basketball, Reggie? The refs have definitely lost control today."

Coach Johnson ran out onto the floor. He and most of my teammates circled above me. The tournament trainer came over.

"I'm fine. I'm fine," I said over the lingering chants of "U.S.A." But I wasn't fine.

I hurt everywhere.

I hurt *everywhere*.

When I finally got up, some of the crowd applauded. It was comforting that some people in the gym cared about me.

"Do you feel well enough to play?" the trainer asked. I looked up at Will's cronies. They didn't seem to be letting up. I spotted Mom talking to the campus security officer, pointing at the stands. Sean rushed over to the area behind our basket. He ripped the poster out of Mike's hands and rushed away.

I left the court without answering the trainer's question and without assistance.

"Where are you going?" Drew yelled after me.

I went straight to Coach.

"I'm done," I said.

"All right, we'll sub someone in while you take a break." He motioned for Will.

"No. Get them out of here, or I walk off." I kept my back to the stands.

Coach looked at me, eyebrows raised and mouth open. You'd think I'd asked him to rob a bank with me or to move to Antarctica. The game came before any of his players. But he called a time-out and went to talk to the refs. Will's pals in the crowd noticed the security officer headed their way. They took off their beards and hurried to the exit.

"What? You can't take a joke?" Eric yelled out from half-court.

"I trash talked in my day, Kevin. But I never stooped so low. Not even against the Knicks, and they had it coming."

I turned toward Eric and charged him.

Drew got in in front of me, blocking Eric from my line of vision. "Forget that guy! He's not worth it."

Marcus and Todd huddled around me, trying to stop me from making a bad decision. Will's friend Steve hung by Coach and the refs, listening to their discussion.

"What do you want to do, Beej?" Marcus asked me.

"I don't want to let you guys down, but I want to leave."

"You won't let us down. Will did, but you won't, no matter what you decide to do."

Coach came back to our bench. He had his hands on his waist and his chin was jutting out like it did when he was stressed at practice.

"There, it's taken care of. Can we get on with basketball now?" Coach said.

I gawked at him. So did Marcus.

"Why are you looking at me like that? You think there aren't going to be creeps in your life? You think you can just run away from them? Let's beat these guys, show them you're not going to let them get to you." Coach was right, but he also didn't know what this felt like. He didn't even seem to care what this felt like. "Now, if you want to sit out a minute, B, that's fine. But we're finishing this game."

"I'll play," I said. "Once you say my name."

"What?" He stared blankly at me as his time-out clock ran down.

"You haven't said my name since I've started playing for you. I don't know if you're embarrassed that you won't pronounce it right or if I'm another anonymous cog in your basketball machine, but I'd like you to say my name before I go out there."

"You are really trying my patience, kid," Coach said.

"It's Bijan, Coach. Not kid," Marcus said. "If he walks, I walk."

"Me too," Todd said.

Coach looked at us like we had lost our minds.

"Say his name," Drew said, looking down at the floor. "It's not that big a deal, Coach." It was the first time I'd ever heard Drew give Coach an opinion.

"Fine. Bijan, if you feel up to playing, I'd really appreciate it." The buzzer sounded on Coach's final word.

I went to the free-throw line to shoot my technical foul. I was alone. The crowd was quiet. The ref bounce-passed me the ball. I tried not to notice the sour faces in the crowd and took my shot. It bounced off the rim.

I took a breath. The ref passed me the ball again. It was just the hoop and me.

In elementary school when other kids left me out, I shot free throws by myself at the park. I'd done this for years.

I dribbled three times, bent my knees, released, and followed through.

The net swished.

I turned around and found Sean's moms jumping up and down in excitement. Sean cheered, his arm around my mom's shoulders. Mom looked at me from her seat, crying. I hadn't seen her do that in years. I hid my face in my jersey so I wouldn't break down on the court.

The horn buzzed for substitutions. Coach was calling me in. Will came on in my place. I walked over to our bench and wiped my eyes. Coach held me by my shoulder.

"Kid . . . Bijan, have a seat," he said softly. "You let me know if you want to go back in again, okay? You want to go in, Will comes right out. He's the substitute here."

I nodded, and he rubbed my back before I took a seat.

From the bench, I watched our slight lead get chipped away and turn into a ten-point deficit. Will kept shooting his infamous jump shot that never fell. The rest of our team looked like they were going through the motions. Even Drew didn't seem to care if we won or lost. They let Will do whatever he wanted, a final display to show him, Mercer

Day, and the crowd that he never made us better, on or off the court.

Our tournament run was over after the first game. All the Granger players except Will and Steve walked off without lining up to shake hands with Mercer Day. As I stood up, Coach put his arm around me, and the two of us walked into the locker room to join the rest of the team.

CHAPTER TWENTY-ONE

Sean spun in my desk chair while I slumped on the edge of my bed. We hung out in my room while our parents talked in hushed tones in the living room.

I had skipped the team bus; Sean rode home with my mom and me after our loss instead of with his parents.

"Can you please put on some music or something?" I asked Sean. I didn't want to hear any murmuring about me.

He quickly obliged and clicked around on my computer. The sound of Andy Shauf filled the room.

I started to sob into my hands. I tried to keep myself quiet. I didn't want to hear my mom, but I didn't want her to hear me either. I felt Sean sit next to me as I let go of all I had been holding inside the past few weeks. I didn't worry about being resilient, about being a good representative for millions of people, about whether I was tough enough or whether people liked me. I let myself feel the anger, the pain, the exhaustion, everything I had been trying to keep at bay.

When the tears subsided, Sean stayed next to me.

"Sorry," I said, wiping my eyes with the end of my sleeve.

"Why?"

"It's embarrassing. Guys don't cry."

"Says you! I'm about to go home and have a good old-fashioned weep myself," Sean said. "Girls love that stuff. Sensitive, brooding types are in now."

I chuckled and took a deep, ragged breath.

"Don't ever change, Sean. You're one of the all-time greats," I said, settling down. "Thanks for taking that poster away from that jerk."

"You'd do it for me, right?"

"Yeah. Of course I would."

"So no sweat. I was going to trash it, but Mama told me to hold on to it in case you need it for evidence. Mom took a video of those morons too," Sean said.

"Will must have forwarded those guys the email," I said.

"I thought so, but then I looked at the poster more closely and it's a different photo of you. Same awful sentiment, but it isn't your old freshman directory photo." He pinched my cheek as though he were my grandmother. "You're growing up so fast. It looked like it was from this year."

"Was it from this year's directory photo?" I asked.

"No. It was higher quality than that. Not so pixelated. It looked like a yearbook portrait."

I blinked a few times. "Are you sure?"

"Pretty sure. But you could ask Elle to double-check."

* * *

I didn't go to school on Monday or Tuesday. I needed a few days to collect myself, but I also needed some time to gather information. I called Elle to confirm that the poster photo matched the one for the yearbook. I had Sean take a photo of the poster to send to Elle because I couldn't bring myself to look at it. I also asked Elle who on the yearbook staff had access to the photos.

My mom fielded a bunch of phone calls that I didn't feel like answering, from teachers, guys from the team, Coach, and some parents. One person didn't call; she just invited herself over.

Our intercom buzzed.

"Hello?" my mom said into the intercom. It killed me that she had a tremor of worry in her voice.

"Hello, this is Stephanie Bergner. I'm a friend of Bijan's from school," the crackly voice said.

"Oh, hi, Stephanie," Mom said. She took her finger off the talk button and looked at me. "Is it okay for her to come up?"

I nodded. Mom smiled at me and pushed the button again.

"Come on up," Mom said into the intercom. She took the chain off our door and opened it, waiting for Stephanie. I put my fingers through my hair, trying to straighten up a little bit. I hadn't showered that morning and was wearing my old moth-eaten Celtics sweatpants and a Captain America T-shirt.

"Hello, Dr. Majidi. I'm Stephanie Bergner. It's very nice to meet you." She stuck her hand out for my mom to shake.

Mom hugged her.

"I know who you are, sweetheart," Mom said, pulling her close. "How are you?"

"I'm okay," Stephanie said as my mom let her go, a little taken aback by her show of affection. "How are you?" she asked, looking at me.

"I'm okay too," I said with a shrug.

My mom invited Stephanie to stay for dinner. At the table, Stephanie didn't ask if the salad was organic like she would at the cafeteria or if the juice came from a major food corporation that exploited migrant laborers.

My mom told Stephanie Coach Johnson had called to tell her that he and my teammates had met with Headmaster Clarkson to go over the events at the Mercer Day game and explain Will Thompson's involvement. Coach had promised Mom that disciplinary action was being taken, though we didn't know the full extent of Will's punishment.

I didn't talk about how I was doing, and neither of them pushed me to.

"Would it be okay, Dr. Majidi, if I spoke to Bijan in private?" Stephanie asked.

"Of course. Come over any time you like," my mom said. Stephanie and I put our plates and cutlery in the dishwasher before I led her to my room.

"When do you think you'll be back at school?" Stephanie asked after I closed my door. I was glad she didn't comment on my *Sports Illustrated* Gigi Hadid poster. I hoped she didn't think I objectified women. Maybe she could appreciate the poster too.

"Tomorrow," I said.

"Good. I miss having my friends at school. Even though I want him out of my life, I even miss Noah. Though I suppose we were never really friends if he could do what he did to me."

"Erin hasn't come back yet?"

Stephanie paused for a moment. "No. She hasn't."

"Have you talked to her?"

"Yes. She's . . . been brief but reassures me that she'll be coming back soon. I spoke with her mother on the phone this afternoon, but she said Erin wasn't in. She was a bit curt with me." Stephanie looked down at her hands. "I don't think her parents were thrilled about their daughter dating the tutor they paid for." She became quiet. Stephanie was petite, that wasn't news, but she'd never looked as small as she did in my room. "I hope that stays between us. I'm sure everyone already assumes she and I are . . . something, but

I'm not sure what Erin will decide to do." She took a deep breath and exhaled. "Are you, um . . . do you still want to be friends? I mean, are you okay with—"

I took her hand in mine.

"We're in this for the long haul, Bergner," I said.

Her lip quivered and she held back tears.

"I know I can be . . . intense," she said. "I never used to mind what people thought about me. When it came time for student council elections, of course I wondered a little about my reputation among my peers, but I mostly focused on the task at hand. Things I was interested in or skills I wanted to improve upon."

I didn't interrupt her. I let her take her time. I listened. That's what friends are supposed to do.

"Then I met this person . . . whom I didn't think much of. But we . . . well, I found myself in the precarious position of falling in love. I really did everything to avoid it. Love, I mean. That avoidance stems from many things: my parents' divorce; how society values couples and coupledom over single people, which I find distressing; how much work it entails to foster a relationship. With everything I do, I don't have much time for myself or anyone else." She cleared her throat, fighting tears that she had no reason to be ashamed of.

"But now, since being with Erin . . . knowing what it's like to feel that kind of happiness, that makes me rethink everything. Our love is so . . . so contained. It can be so *difficult* sometimes because of how different we are. Now all I can think about is other people, how they view me."

She stopped talking and took a few more breaths.

I let go of her hand and took a moment to think about what I could say after hearing about everything she was going through.

"I don't know much about romance," I said. "I guess, it's just women are so, um . . . well, you guys—not guys, your *people*, girls—are very enigmatic."

"My *people*?" she asked with a laugh. I was glad my incompetence in the romance department gave her a little break from her heartache.

"Women! Women people! I know I'm bad at this," I said. I let out a small, awkward chortle.

"I suppose I should save all this for Ms. Jacobs," Stephanie said, laughing while taking a travel pack of Kleenex from her pocket. She dabbed the corners of her eyes with a tissue.

"You are definitely not the kind of person who should be kept secret. In my opinion, no one should, but you especially. You know that. You don't need me to tell you, but maybe love makes people forget themselves sometimes."

Stephanie looked at me like she'd never seen me before but was suddenly pleased that she had. "I *am* extraordinary."

"Modest too. Don't forget modest," I said. We were quiet for a moment. "So are you excited to be a representative for a minority population?"

"No. Have any pointers?"

"It's always good to have people around who support you. Even if they may not know how to go about supporting you right away."

She nodded. "You're pretty extraordinary too," she said. "I'm not the only one who thinks so. I brought you a present." She pulled a wrapped gift from her backpack.

"What's this?" I asked. I opened it up and found a blue plush official NBA doll of G-Wiz, the Washington Wizards mascot.

"The board has agreed to meet again in a month to debate the pros and cons of changing the mascot. They are also open to new ideas for what the mascot should be if they decide to change it. I know you have mixed feelings about the campaign, and rightfully so, but if you ever want to help us brainstorm, we could use your expertise." She pointed to the toy I'd pulled out of the box. "The Washington team used to be called the Bullets," she continued. "Seems as though they understood something the Granger administration doesn't."

"Seems so," I said, holding up my new furry friend. Even though G-Wiz didn't rep my team, the little blue toy would be one of my most prized possessions. "Though we have to come up with something better than this guy."

"I think we can manage that."

CHAPTER TWENTY-TWO

Charlie Martin got out of his seat yet again when he saw
Sean and me walk into the auditorium for assembly.

"Hey, guys," he said warmly. "Glad to see you back,
Bijan."

"Thanks, Charlie," I said.

Sean looked over at the senior section as we sat down.
"I still don't see Will," he said. "I bet he's been booted."

I didn't want to get my hopes up. While Will was a complete jerk, he wasn't the one who had sent the email.

The bell rang to signal the beginning of the assembly. A
few dawdlers rushed to their seats as the audience quieted
down. One latecomer didn't rush. She walked slowly and
deliberately into the auditorium, with everyone watching
her.

"She's back," Sean whispered, staring at Erin Wheeler. Erin didn't head to her seat behind us. Instead, she marched to Stephanie's row.

"Uh-oh. We may be about to witness a throwdown of epic proportions, Reggie."

Stephanie looked up from her seat to find a smiling Erin. She stood up but hesitated, like she didn't know what to do or say. Then Erin hugged her in front of the whole school.

"Would you listen to that crowd? They are loving this adorable but unlikely duo, Kevin."

"Doesn't look like everyone is loving them together, Reggie. Check out the grimace on Jessica Carter!"

"I see it. I don't like it, but I see it."

Erin let go of Stephanie and smiled at her before she went back to her seat. Stephanie turned around and looked at Sean and me, grinning like a kid going to Disneyland. We each gave her two thumbs-ups.

"Nice to see some lovely faces back in the crowd," Ms. McCrea said from the stage. She was tasked with running assembly instead of Headmaster Clarkson, who was busy in his office with the materials Elle and I had sent. "We have a lot on the docket today, so let's begin."

I psyched myself up as assembly continued with scheduled announcements. After the finance club told everyone they'd be discussing early retirement planning at their next meeting, Ms. McCrea looked down at her sheet to see who else was slated to speak.

"Bijan," she said.

Sean turned to me with raised eyebrows.

"Now, Bijan absolutely hates public speaking. He probably hates public speaking as much as DeAndre Jordan hates shooting free throws."

"There goes our superstar, lumbering onto the stage with the grace of a baby elephant trying to walk for the first time."

"He's nervous, Kevin. Cut him some slack."

"Uh, hi," I said, looking out at a sea of faces. From up onstage, it seemed like the school's population had doubled. I did my best not to look anyone directly in the eyes.

"My name's Bijan," I said with a nervous chuckle. "You may have seen me around campus recently. I'm not really great at making speeches, but I wanted to say a few things." I pulled a folded piece of paper from my pocket. "So, um, a little about me. I love basketball. I like to read, mostly sports memoirs, graphic novels, and Stephen King books. My favorite is *Christine*, even though the premise of a killer car is a little over-the-top. My favorite sandwich is peanut butter and jelly, which some might find basic, but I think it's a classic choice."

I looked up at the audience. "And I'm not a terrorist." I looked back down at my paper. "I live in Somerville. I've got good friends who have really shown up for me these past few weeks. I think I'd like to pursue sports journalism in college, even though my mom says there's no money in it. And I'm not a terrorist."

I paused again. The audience probably thought it was for dramatic effect, but I was mostly trying to steady my breathing. I hoped I wouldn't pass out.

"I have a wonderful mom who was raised by her wonderful parents, who are originally from Iran. My dad passed away when I was a kid, but he was originally from Jordan. They aren't terrorists.

"My mom is Muslim but doesn't speak to God much since my dad died. My father was Christian. My relationship with God is personal and has nothing to do with you. Nor is it my job to explain the geopolitics of countries you keep hearing about in the news or to defend a peaceful religion practiced by one-point-six billion people. I'm a sixteen-year-old student, and I don't have all the answers you want me to have."

I didn't explain to them that no Iranian had yet committed an act of terror in the United States, nor had Iran invaded any other country in an unjust war. I didn't explain to them that Jordan is a longtime partner in working on counterterrorism with the U.S. I didn't explain to them that terrorists who commit heinous acts in the name of religion don't understand their faith at all, including the white Christian terrorists within our own country.

I didn't read to them the section of the Qur'an that says, "Whoever kills a person unjustly . . . it is as though he has killed all mankind, and whoever saves a life, it is as though he had saved all mankind."

Maybe I should have told them all that. But would they have cared?

"I want to thank those of you who have made me feel comfortable or checked in on me." I kept my eyes fixed on my paper. No one had booed me yet, so I was doing okay. "To the person who sent that email of me," I said, "I'm not going to cower or allow ignorance to run my life. I'm going to be me, whether you like it or not." Now I stared at Jessica.

She scowled at me, her arms folded across her chest.

"Unlike our dumb mascot, I *am* here to stay. I'm not going anywhere."

I finally looked out into the whole crowd. "So that's all I wanted to say. Thanks."

I walked back to my seat.

"Would you listen to that crowd, Reggie? They are making noise for Majidi. I haven't heard this kind of uproar since the 1986 NBA finals in the Garden!"

"Our little guy is growing up."

Sean gave me a one-man standing ovation. "That's my brother from another mother right there!" he yelled, pointing.

I blushed profusely but did my best not to slump in my chair. I waited for everyone to stop clapping. It was nice of them, but I'd had enough attention to last a lifetime. I needed to get all that out once and for all. I peered over the seats in front of me at Jessica Carter, three rows ahead. She wasn't clapping.

When Ms. McCrea ended assembly, I stayed in my seat.

"You need backup?" Sean asked. One day, I hoped I'd be able to show Sean how much I appreciated his friendship. I think going to his art show with a poster that reads *Eye of the Tiger, Sean* might be a good place to start.

"No, thanks. I got this," I said. He ruffled my hair and left the auditorium with everyone else—everyone except Jessica, who sat in her seat, staring at the empty stage. We both waited until we were the only two people left.

"That was quite the speech," Jessica said without looking at me. "A little hokey, but not bad."

"I haven't had a lot of practice having to defend my humanity," I replied. "Hopefully I won't have to do it again."

She rotated in her seat and watched me. I leaned over, hoping I appeared a hundred times more casual than I felt, and rested my arms and chin on the back of the seat in front of me.

"Any idea why Ms. McCrea was running assembly instead of Headmaster Clarkson this morning? Or why Elle texted me last night asking if I had anything I wanted to tell her?"

"I think I have an idea," I said. "I think you do too. Or you wouldn't be sitting here."

"Maybe I enjoy your company."

"I find that difficult to believe. You went to all that trouble to make my life hell."

Her mouth twitched. She may have wanted to smile, then thought better of it.

"If Mr. Clarkson thought I was responsible, what proof would he have?"

"He might have some evidence from the yearbook staff. From one amazing star photographer in particular. Knowing your ex-boyfriend's character, to save his own skin, he'd probably confess to Coach Johnson in a heartbeat who lent her artistic skills to making those posters for the Mercer Day game. He'd probably have some emails sent from you to show off too."

Her cheeks reddened. Maybe it was dawning on her what everyone else knew: Will Thompson wasn't loyal to anyone but himself. Still, she didn't break.

"Did he tell you to do that to me?" I asked her.

"Hypothetically speaking?"

I nodded. *Sure, Lady Death Strike. Hypothetically speaking.*

"He was worried you might take his playing time. And since you showed up," she said, like I hadn't been going to this school and I hadn't been in her grade for three years, "Erin's crying over Busted Bergner and doesn't have time for me, Elle is trying to change our mascot, you're pulling my crew into your parking-lot brawls . . . School used to be awesome. Now it's like—it's like I don't recognize it anymore. And everyone's obsessed with you. You didn't know your place."

"My place? And you decided you could fix that with that photo?"

"So big deal, it was a dumb photo. Do you think people were upset by that email? The people I heard from felt satisfied." She paused to brush back a piece of her hair. "I see what's happening in the news. Why should I have to pretend that I'm fine with you going to school here?"

"What's happening in the news, Jessica?" I asked through gritted teeth.

"There's a holy war, in case you haven't noticed," she spat.

"There are wars, but they have as much to do with power and money and resources as with religion," I said. "You think we would have an interest in controlling the Middle East if there weren't oil there?"

"That's very cute, how you say 'we,'" she said with a smirk. "Like it's your country."

I leaned back in my seat, studying her face for any tics or any remorse for what she'd just said. There weren't any. She meant every word that came out of her mouth.

"Since you know so much about terrorists, you probably know a whole lot about the KKK. Or do you have Klansmen relatives, so they don't count?" I asked her.

Jessica rolled her eyes.

"I feel sick to my stomach when innocent people die," I said. "Whether they're killed in a movie theater, a school, or a drone strike, it makes me ill. I mourn when anyone is killed. Here or elsewhere."

"That's your problem. What is that supposed to mean? 'Here or elsewhere'? You've got to pick a side," Jessica said. "No one can tell whose side you're on."

Teams. In Jessica's mind, humanity was split up into teams. I got out of my seat and left her alone. There wouldn't be any reasoning with her.

I didn't want the anger I'd felt the past few weeks, the pain she'd caused, to change me. I didn't want hate to feel like a constant hum inside me, making me question every friend I had, every conversation, wondering if someone was going to do something horrible to me just for existing in the same space. I didn't want to give her that power. I walked out of the auditorium to the mostly empty hallway.

Elle was waiting for me.

"Hey," she said.

"Hi." I was happy to see her, and I wanted to smile for her, but I was drained to nothing. "Aren't you going to be late for class?"

"Mr. Clarkson gave some of the yearbook staff notes for first period," she said. "We just finished up in his office. I heard you made a speech."

"Your presentation inspired me." I took a deep breath. "I need to ask you something," I said, looking down at the floor. Elle reached over and took my hand, and I looked up into her eyes. "Did you, um, did you know what Jessica was like?"

She didn't answer right away.

"I think Erin knew more than I did," she finally said. "Jessica was always pretty careful with the way she spoke around me. Wonder why." She paused again. "It freaks me out, though. We've been friendly for years, but I don't know if we were ever truly friends. To be friends you actually have to know someone, right? Most of the time we'd talk about yearbook, boys, music, but I never spoke with her about things that were really important to me. Maybe she liked it better that way."

I couldn't shake the things Jessica had said to me a few minutes earlier. I knew she was wrong, but no one was going to change her mind—at least, not anytime soon.

"Are you okay?" Elle asked.

"I'm . . . I think I am some days," I said. "Others, I want to get as far away from here as possible, move to some remote island. Then I think there's really nowhere like that to go, and I don't really want to hide anymore. But I definitely don't want to make speeches every week."

"I can't imagine why not. You always know the right thing to say." It actually felt nice to be teased a little, especially with Elle doing the teasing.

"I want to get back to thinking about whether I'm going to pass my math test, what movie Sean and I should see over the weekend, who's going to make the NBA All-Star team, what I should say when I bump into you so I don't sound like a total babbling weirdo . . ." At least she didn't seem to mind my babbling. "I want to *stop* thinking about my mom crying. She thinks she can protect me forever, but she can't. We both know that, but we can't say it to each other."

"How come?"

"I think deep down, we have a feeling things are actually getting worse, and it's too scary to think about," I said. "Sean says it's the Age of the Assholes."

"Oh, they've always been around," Elle said. "This might be new for you, but they never go out of style. Trust me, I've got some stories."

"I'd like to hear them," I said. "Any of your stories. Good or bad, I'd like to know."

Elle leaned up and kissed me. I cupped her face in my hand. She was so warm. Kissing her was a million times better than scoring the winning basket for Granger.

When she backed away, she put her hand on my chest. "I believe you would," she said.

CHAPTER TWENTY-THREE

My mom and I were asked to come to Headmaster Clarkson's office two days after I confronted Jessica. Everyone from our previous meeting was there except Mr. Thompson. After Will's fall from grace, he probably wouldn't be making many appearances on the Granger campus for a while. Coach Johnson was at this meeting too. He didn't look so stressed now that basketball season was over.

"Ms. Powell, as well as the school's IT department, confirmed for me that the yearbook staff have individual logins," Headmaster Clarkson said. "Meaning these photographs of Bijan were available only to the photo editors. We also verified that there were two photos used for the posters at the Mercer Day game and both came from the yearbook drive.

"Will Thompson confirmed that he had the original email in his possession before it was sent to the student body as a whole, sent to him from an email address belonging to Ms. Carter."

I bet Coach Johnson was instrumental in convincing Will to turn in his girlfriend. That must be some new kind of low, but Will still needed an in at Trinity. Maybe he'd write an essay about how he used to bully a kid but then learned a lesson about why isms and bullying are bad. Colleges love that stuff. He'd be fine.

"Ms. Carter is no longer a student here," Headmaster Clarkson continued.

"Good," Mom said, her hand over mine as we sat in chairs next to each other. I didn't pull my hand away. "Did she apologize? Did her parents apologize?"

"On behalf of the Granger School, I would like to apologize to you both," Headmaster Clarkson said. I took that to mean the Carters hadn't said they were sorry about anything. "Especially for assuming Noah Olson was responsible for all the cyber-related offenses and not investigating further after his expulsion."

"What can we do to make sure something like this doesn't happen again?" Mom asked. "What can we do about the images of my son that may exist online, which college admissions boards might find in a quick web search without knowing the context? What about the damage that's been done to his spirit?"

"Unfortunately, we cannot control what may take place off campus," Mr. Clarkson said. This seemed to be his go-to line, reiterating that the school wasn't technically at fault. The school probably had attorneys telling him to avoid accepting responsibility. "But we do have some programs on the horizon to foster a better sense of community."

"We have scheduled a full day of workshops in April to address the emotional needs of the students," Ms. Jacobs said. "We will discuss bullying prevention and conduct exercises to help build bridges between students from different social circles."

Most kids would probably be stoked to get out of classes and tests. Maybe by the end of the day, we'd all be singing folk songs and playing Frisbee. Get a good game of Frolf going with your secretly bigoted classmate!

"Majidi's still a little bitter, Reggie."

"I think that's all right for now, Kevin. So long as it doesn't eat away at him like McNair's ex-wife in Zombie Killers Part Three.*"*

"Was it part three or part four?"

"No idea. This is Bijan's train of thought. I haven't seen any of them—too much violence for my moviegoing sensibilities. Now let's hear a word from our sponsor, Zombie Killers Part Six.*"*

"There are going to be changes at Granger. We can assure you of that," Ms. McCrea promised. As usual, she had an optimistic outlook, with no concrete evidence to back up her vision. I still owed her my paper, but she hadn't brought it up again.

"That's all very well and good, Ms. McCrea," Mom said. "While I'm happy that steps are being taken to change the culture here at Granger, I wonder if maybe your curriculum could use some changes as well."

"I don't follow," Mr. Clarkson said.

"The text for your world history class. Bijan showed it to me. It's dated, and frankly, it offers a fairly one-sided perspective. The books from Bijan's English class are also limited in perspective. I understand the students need to be prepared for tests and higher education, and I am sure there are constraints on teachers, but the students here should go into the world having a fuller understanding of American and global history and culture. The history of every kind of student here, and also the history of people they will encounter after they leave Granger."

"I think that's a fine idea and something we can look into over the summer," Mr. Clarkson said. By the time they got around to implementing that, I would probably be in graduate school—or a retirement home.

"Speaking of summer," Coach interjected, "your son has real talent on the basketball court, Mrs. Majidi. I run a camp over at Regis College and would love to have Bijan train with us. If I work with B, I think he'd have a great season next year and possibly attract the attention of some college scouts."

"We'll discuss it when we get home," Mom said, looking from him to me a little warily.

"Are there any other Granger kids there?" I asked. No matter how awful this season had been, the idea of playing basketball all summer appealed to me.

"The only other Granger student there will be Drew Young. The other players come from all over."

I could tell my mom wasn't crazy about the idea, but at this point I could have asked to eat ice cream every night for dinner and she'd have let me.

"We'll think about it," my mom said to Coach.

The bell rang and my mom shook hands with all the teachers. She was making a follow-up appointment with Headmaster Clarkson when I approached the guidance counselor outside Mr. Clarkson's office.

"Ms. Jacobs?" I asked.

She turned around, a little startled.

"Uh, hi."

"Bijan, hi," she said.

"Your office is, um . . . it's upstairs, away from the masses?"

I didn't know where to go from there. She didn't smile at me condescendingly or anything like that, which was good. I wasn't sold on visiting the school counselor, but Stephanie said seeing Ms. Jacobs was helping her. Maybe talking to an objective person could do something for me too, even if I didn't always have the right words.

"Yes. It's very discreet. As are the conversations in my office."

"Okay. Cool, cool." I didn't elaborate, but I knew how to find her if I felt like I needed to. "I heard you have snacks up there. So . . ."

"There are snacks," she confirmed. This time she smiled a little.

I nodded and gave her a small wave, bowing out of our conversation.

I stepped into the hallway, where students were rushing to get to their classes. Stephanie, Erin, Elle, and Sean walked over, trying to act as if they hadn't been loitering there, waiting for me to show up.

"What's going on?" I asked.

"I told them your mom was going to be here and Stephanie just *had* to say hello again," Sean said.

"Someone else was curious to meet her too," Erin said. Elle looked nervous and elbowed Erin. How did Elle continue to get more adorable than was humanly possible?

Mom came out of the office to join us.

"Hi, Dr. M," Sean said.

"Hello, Sean. Stephanie, nice to see you again." Mom looked relieved to see some familiar faces.

"It's very nice to see you again, Dr. Majidi," Stephanie said. "This is my—this is Erin." It was kind of amazing to watch the pink rise from her neck to her hairline as she spoke.

"Her girlfriend," Erin said, with all the confidence of her years in the New Crew. She reached out to shake my mom's hand. "Hi. Your son is a stand-up guy."

"Thank you for saying so. I think he's quite a stand-up guy myself."

When Erin let go of my mom's hand, she took Stephanie's in its place.

"Mom, this is Elle Powell," I said, scooting to stand next to Elle so I could properly introduce her.

"I'm so very happy to meet you, Elle," Mom said. "You were wonderful at the meeting with the board. Bijan has always spoken so highly of you."

"He has, huh?" Erin asked, and this time Stephanie elbowed her.

"It's nice to meet you too," Elle said, blushing as much as I was.

"Thank you so much for all your help," my mom said, hugging Elle supertight. I was mortified. Elle didn't seem to mind, though. She hugged my mom right back.

CHAPTER TWENTY-FOUR

"Majidi is on the attack! The shot clock is winding down, the game is tied up, he's on a fast streak to the hoop, and BANG! He's won the game for the Boston Celtics!"

"Are you kidding me? This is unbelievable! The fans are going wild!"

"This was the kind of performance people will be talking about for years. The Celtics are NBA champions once again!"

"Hey!" Drew shouted at me. He had changed into gym clothes, but I was still in my school uniform, tie and everything. I was goofing around, shooting hoops by myself, waiting for Sean to get out of the ceramics studio so I could hitch a ride home. Drew, with his own basketball under his arm, looked ready to work.

"Hi. Do you have the gym reserved or something?"

"No. You can shoot around." He dribbled up to where I stood at the top of the key. He released his ball and missed, the clanging of the rim the only noise in the whole gym.

I shot my ball and missed too. We both ran to get our own rebounds.

"We could use the one ball," Drew suggested.

"Okay."

He shot, missed, got his rebound, and tried again. He missed. I got the ball, threw it. It bounced off the rim and fell in.

"Made baskets get the ball," Drew said, passing the rock to me. I dribbled, released, got rewarded with the rock again.

I airballed. Drew chased after it. He dribbled between his legs before shooting a floater in the paint. He made it.

"Coach said you're thinking about camp this summer," Drew said.

"Thinking about it," I said, passing the ball to him. "You worried I'm going to take your spot or something?"

"No. I'm too good. But it'd be all right to room together."

"Why?" I asked. He threw up a brick. "Aren't you mad I ruined the tournament for us?"

"We wouldn't have even gotten to the tournament if it wasn't for you." Drew passed me the ball. "The seniors are leaving, and it'll be up to us to lead the team next year. You're not bad. You're not great, but you're not bad."

"What a sad vote of confidence, Reggie."

"Shhh! I think they're bonding. In their own macho, elusive way."

"Why don't people say how they feel anymore, Reggie? I mean, we certainly do."

"That's because we're paid to."

"Thanks. I guess," I said, slamming the ball down with both hands. It shot up over my head. "I bet I could take you one-on-one." I caught the ball.

"You could. But you'd lose," Drew said.

"Want to find out?" I sent him a bounce pass.

"Okay," he said, moving to the top of the key.

Drew and I played until we were both soaked with sweat. When he tried to fake me out, I wouldn't fall for it. When I tried to steal the ball from him, he'd cross over and breeze on by to the hoop. By the time we were tied up at 20 apiece, I was exhausted. He might have been too, but he didn't let on.

"How about next point wins?" I asked.

"Fine by me," Drew said. He had the ball, backing into me as he dribbled. "What do you think we'll be called next year? The Granger Sea Lions or some other animal Bergner is trying to save?"

"I do like Sea Lions," I said as he pushed into me. "But I don't think that's going to work."

Drew dribbled until he had enough room to turn around. He took a shot. I boxed out and scooped up his miss. Drew was intense, but he looked like he was having fun, like he had strayed from his typical practice routine to play and show off.

I squared up against him.

"What are you going to do?" Drew asked me as he reached in for the ball.

I was going to live my life. I was going to spend time with people who cared about me and whom I cared about. I was going to be comfortable in my own skin even when some people wanted to make that impossible for me.

I was also going to score a layup on Drew's punk ass.

"Bijan surges forward! He's a man with a plan, with his eye on the sky, and BANG! He scores!"

"I think Bijan Majidi has a bright future ahead of him, Kevin. Not as bright as my career, mind you, but he's going to go a long way."

"I hope so, Reggie. I really do hope so."

ACKNOWLEDGMENTS

Bijan's story took a lot out of me and would not have been possible without the following people:

My father and mother, to whom I owe so much and whose unconditional love and support always makes me feel so incredibly lucky and grateful. They taught me to be proud of who I am and I could not be more proud of who they are. My uncles, Kian and Shahab, for watching Celtics games with me from the eighties until now. My grandmother, who introduces me as a writer to random strangers and who helped raise me on stories of her past. My sister, for making me laugh and making sure I don't take things too seriously. Elise Howard, my fairy godmother, who still believes in me and my characters. Thank you, Elise, for your patience and for seeing this story through. Susan Ginsburg, for being a wonderful agent and taking me on as a client. Sarah Alpert, for her editing assistance over multiple drafts. I owe you big-time! Brooke Csuka, Ashley Mason, Jodie Cohen, Caitlin Rubinstein, Jacquelynn Burke, Eileen Lawrence, Trevor Ingerson, and all past and present Algonquin Young Readers team members and authors. My mentor, Chris Lynch, for asking me what I'm working on even when I don't have an answer. Thank you for always asking, Chris. Jacqui Bryant, for getting me back in the writing groove and for finding me a day job that accommodates my writing. Day job friends, for computer research questions and listening to my writing nonsense, particularly Pavani, Sumit, Paul, Liz, Amy, Kat, Kate, and George. Marisa Pintado, for reading an early draft and for being the kindest person I've ever met. Jessica Spotswood, Saundra Mitchell, and Lamar Giles, for inviting me to write stories for their awesome anthologies. Maggie Tokuda-Hall, who is the coolest; the crew of Books Inc. Laurel Village circa 2013–2014 (love you all); Maria Loli Reyes, Kaveh, Kevin, Marmar, Rana, Laura Kinney, Steve from Outer Limits Comics, Jessica Golden-Weaver, Malinda Lo, Meredith Goldstein, Leila, Carolina, Christina, and Steph. I owe all of you and many other friends and family so much.

I want to thank all the teachers, librarians, booksellers, students, bloggers, authors, and journalists who have supported me over the years. And dear reader, I want to thank you so very much for finding this book. Bijan's story is just one story and he's not perfect. He is sixteen and doesn't have all the answers, but he's trying to figure out who he is in the world without others defining him. I hope his story resonates with you and that he's a hero you want to root for.

SARA FARIZAN is an Iranian American writer and ardent basketball fan who was born in and lives near Boston. The award-winning author of *If You Could Be Mine* and *Tell Me Again How a Crush Should Feel*, she has an MFA from Lesley University and a BA in film and media studies from American University. *Here to Stay* is her third novel.